THE MAN IN THE FROOPY HAT

Written By
Tanner Howsden

Published by Incalescent Productions

Cover design by A.A. Medina
(https://fabledbeastdesign.myportfolio.com/)

Trigger Warnings:
- Schizophrenia
- Mental Health Hospitals
- Child Abuse

Dedicated to everyone who has ever seen the Hat Man and wondered about his life. Who is he? Why does he show up? What does he want? Is he friend or foe?

May we all someday find the answers we seek.

We are but dust and shadow.

HORACE

CONTENTS

When the dark ones grow fat
From their invisible chat
Find the man in the hat

Hear the walls lie with blame
Bury all with false shame
When the dark ones grow fat

Bringing you to your least
On your tears, they thus feast
Find the man in the hat

They bore into your soul
Leaving you never whole
When the dark ones grow fat

In a breath, voices fade
With a flick of his blade
Find the man in the hat

As your mind becomes clean
Never again is he seen
When the dark ones grow fat
Find the man in the hat

- R. Steinlin

CHAPTER 1

"AAAAAA! No! Shut up! Go away! Shut up! Shut up! SHUT UP!!!"

From just down the hall, I hear a woman's voice exhaustively crying out with a familiar shriek of pain. She sounds young, probably no more than 10 or 12 years old.

"Oh my god, they're so loud! Please! Make them stop! Make them stop! Make them STOP!!!"

With each shriek, I slowly advance toward the sound of her voice, cautiously looking around at my surroundings. I don't want to step into something without knowing the situation.

"June, sweetie," an old man answers with a tone of exasperation, "who are you talking to? It's just the two of us. There's no one else in here."

From the exasperated tone in his voice, I assume this is her father. Every word he speaks is laced with doubt and contrition, as if he's already diagnosed his daughter's mental condition and her prospects for recovery.

"NO! You're wrong!! Listen!! Can't you hear

them all around us?!?"

"Sweetie," he says again, desperately searching for a quick solution to her woes rather than listening to her words. "I told you, no one else is here. Look around. Do you actually see anyone else around us?"

Part of me wants to scream at this man. Of course she can't see the voices. No one can. It would be so much easier if she could.

In all fairness, were I in his position during my mortal years, I might have thought the same thing. It's hard to believe in the existence of a creature that you can't see or hear.

Yet, just because he can't hear them doesn't mean they aren't screaming at her. Terrorizing her. Haunting her every waking thought, turning even the most docile of times into a living nightmare.

"They...they're just so loud!" The girl's voice snaps with an anxious tone. "Can't you hear them?!? They're here!! They're here!! I'm telling you...oh no. They're right, aren't they?!? You don't trust me, do you?!?"

"My little June bug." His tone is soft and caring, but clearly doubtful and dismissive. "I will always trust you. But look around us. There's no one else here right now. This is just another one of your episodes."

One of her...episodes? Every judgemental

word this horrid man speaks makes me feel a little queasier.

Of course he thinks it's just the two of them. No surprise there. Every parent thinks it's just them and their child, never that the child sees or hears something more.

It's always the same. As much as family and friends want to help, they never see the truth from beyond the veil. All they ever see is their precious daughter or friend struggling against her mind.

They never see the fiends who come to haunt the troubled and feast on their pain.

They never hear the demons surrounding their poor children, yelling constant streams of demeaning obscenities and terrifying lies in their ears.

All they ever see is the mask of the convenient lie that is insanity covering up the nature of their child's true demons.

"See? He absolutely knows you're crazy," a soft slow demonic voice hisses in the background. "He doesn't know what to do with you, so he's going to tell everyone what a disappointment you are and lock you in here forever and ever."

"Why wouldn't he? Look at yourself!" The second demonic voice is sharper and raspier with a fiery edge. "LOOK AT YOURSELF! See what you've made him do to you! This is ALL your fault, you spineless LOSER!"

I'd recognize those foul, treacherous voices anywhere. Sorrowsworn. Horrible, twisted demonic beings who visit the mortal plain solely to feast upon the fear and suffering of young children. Emotional leeches who know how to drive pain with sharp lies.

There's only one way to deal with creatures like that, I tell myself as I feel the cold metallic blade of my knife resting anxiously in my belt.

"Is there a doctor nearby?" the girl's father yells out into the hallway. "We need someone in here right now!"

"My my," answers the voice of the first Sorrowsworn for the girl's ears only. "He certainly seems anxious to get rid of you, doesn't he?"

A tall blonde woman in a lab coat rushes urgently towards the screaming child, oblivious enough to my presence to dash straight through my ethereal body.

She looks slightly familiar, but I don't immediately recognize her face. If she's anything like the rest of the doctors here, it'll just be a matter of time until she tries to prescribe a litany of pills and hope the problem magically goes away.

When I approach the room, I see the doctor standing next to a young girl, looking at a clipboard. The girl is sitting in a chair, staring at a white wall on the opposite side of the room with a fearful, unblinking expression across her face.

“Are you June Murphy?” the doctor asks.

The child barely nods as a quiet tear runs down her cheek.

“Pleasure to meet you. I’m Dr. Dawn Heaton. I would like to try to help you if I can.” I watch as the doctor sets down her clipboard and kneels at the child’s side, offering her right hand in support. “What seems to be the problem?”

“I don’t know, doctor,” June’s father starts. “After her cousin Sebastian ran—"

“Shut it!” Dr. Heaton’s words cut him off before a full thought escapes his lips. “I want to hear about her experience, not yours.”

June’s father starts to protest, but quickly swallows his words as the doctor’s left hand flies up at him.

Impressive. Maybe this doctor will be better than the rest.

“June, how are you doing?”

As June starts to speak, I walk slowly into the room and try to get a better view, doing what I can to stay out of sight. If she is like others I have met in the past, then she’ll be able to see me, but not hear me. Conversely she’ll be able to hear the Sorrowsworn, but not see them.

Being yelled at by voices you can't see which constantly belittle and scream at you just to feed off of your pain sounds like the worst kind of curse.

Sliding closer, I glimpse two Sorrowsworn demons standing right behind her, a red one and a green one at her right and left sides respectively. I'm a bit surprised to only see two. Usually they attack in threes.

"Why don't you tell her what the REAL problem is?" The red demon yells straight into the girl's ear, accentuating the assault upon her mind further. "Tell her that you're a failure failure failure failure failure failure failure FAILURE!!!"

"I bet Aunt Rachel told him what a terrible child you are," the green demon shrieks into her other ear. "He's going to leave you here forever and ever and ever!!"

The poor girl tries to speak, but instead breaks down in tears as the pair of demons savor the flavor in the air of her pain with a light giggle.

"You'll spend eternity sleeping all alone, just like..."

Enough. I'm done with these two. One way or another, they need to go.

I slink into a dark area of the room and stand just behind the green demon, tapping him lightly on the shoulder. Offering him a chance to escape he doesn't deserve.

"Beat it, punk," he answers, not even taking the time to look at me. "Find your own food!"

I pull out my knife and poke his arm with the tip of my blade to further drive home the point. This time, he looks back toward me wearing a face filled with irritation.

"Damn it! This is ours! Get your ow—"

The demon cuts off his words sharply as he takes a look at my visage. I point at the door, offering the demon one last chance to leave. Yet the moment I start to lift the knife toward my throat to show him what will happen if he doesn't listen, my ears ache with the piercing sound of pained screams coming from a child in mortal terror.

"W...who...?" The girl's face fades to a pale shade of white as she taps her father on the chest and then points across the room. "T...that man..."

"Sweetie," her father says while looking around the room with exasperation, "I don't...see anyone. I'm telling you we're the only people here."

"He's going to kill us!!" June's voice starts to crack as she springs from her chair, pulling her hand away from the doctor as she futilely tries to open the now closed door. "We have to run away now!! He wants to kill us! He has a KNIFE!!!!"

I look up from the demon to see what she is seeing. Across the room is a mirror showing her reflection...and me, standing here holding a knife in my hand in the middle of making a throat slitting gesture.

God damn it.

"Take a deep breath," Dr. Heaton says, as if carbon dioxide is a form of protective medicine from knife-wielding maniacs. "Just relax. It's OK. You're safe here."

"SAFE?!?!?" After several attempts to open the door, June falls against it exhausted with fear still encompassing her eyes. "How can you say that?!?!? None of us are safe here with him!"

"June bug." Her father shakes his head in doubt after looking around the room. "There's no one here."

I put away my knife with a regretful sigh, apologetically nodding with a tip of my cap. I hope she understands the gesture.

"He's here!! Right there!!" The child looks up at her father in disbelief, again pointing at my reflection in the mirror. "We have to go!!!"

"Mmmmmmm! Thank you," the green Sorrowsworn says while both demons swiftly float toward the child, savoring every last gasp of her pain in the air. "Good job. You really know how to make a demon feel special!"

Just wait, demon.

"June, I'd like you to meet someone," Dr.

Heaton says as she quietly pulls a small, dirty stuffed elephant out of her left lab coat pocket, placing it in June's lap. "His name is Raul. He's a protector. Would you be willing to let him be your protector?"

"P…protector?" June looks at Dr. Heaton before taking several deep breaths to compose herself. With her gaze turned away from the mirror, I take the opportunity to hide myself. "He can't protect me. He's just a stupid stuffed elephant."

"Ah, but he's so much more," Dr. Heaton answers. "Do you still see that scary man?"

June wipes away a tear from her eyes as she looks around the room. I make sure to stay out of sight, playing along with the charade.

"I…I don't see him," she answers with a bit of hesitation as she looks closer at the elephant. "Was… did I just make him up? Is…is he afraid of…this thing?"

The green demon leans over her ear with a cackling sound.

"He wasn't real, you know. You're just imagining things like the fail—"

Silently from the shadows, my knife does us all the favor of ending the demon's existence. He convulses for a second before vanishing from this plane in a puff of smoke. The red one backs away slowly before fleeing through the nearby wall in fear.

"Maybe," the doctor answers with a smile. "Raul is pretty tough. Can you tell me about the man? What did he look like?"

"For the love of Christ," June's father exclaims. "Why are you encourag—"

Dr. Heaton interrupts him again by raising her hand.

"You can go wait in the hall," she tells him, pointing her finger towards the door. "My patient and I are in the middle of girl talk."

"But..."

"You! Out! Now!"

After a bit of grumbling and eye rolling, he eventually steps out when the doctor threatens to call security. Whether or not anyone would have actually taken him away, the threat is effective enough to push him out of the room for the time being.

"Sorry about that," Dr. Heaton says. "You doing OK? Is Raul doing a good job of protecting you?"

"I...think so?" June starts. "The voices are gone and so is that weird, creepy guy in the hat."

"I'm glad," Dr. Heaton answers. "Raul is a good protector. When I was your age, he gave me the strength I needed."

June smiles as she gives Raul a hug.

"June," Dr. Heaton starts, "can I ask you a question? Nothing severe, just something between us girls?"

"S...sure," June answers, "but I get to ask you something afterwards."

"OK, deal." Dr. Heaton states in agreement. "That guy you saw, the one with the knife. What can you tell me about him? How was he dressed?"

"Well," June offers, "he was standing over by the wall. He was wearing all black from head to toe, including a long flowing trenchcoat and a froopy hat!"

"A...froopy hat? What exactly makes a hat froopy? Like, was it shaped like this?"

June laughs uproariously as Dr. Heaton slumps over several times in various contortions, trying to capture the essence of my worn fedora via charades.

"Well...was he cute?" Dr. Heaton continues. "Should I have a crush on him?"

"Ewwww! No! God no! Gross!" The child answers her with a laugh, probably her first good laugh all day. "You can do so much better than him! His face was all burned and ugly and nasty! He's probably crawling with cooties."

I bite my lip as I depart through the nearby

wall, trying not to take offense as I hear her description of me fade into the distance.

CHAPTER 2

There's something kind of magical about the innocence of youth. If I had to suffer with everything that poor girl has had to deal with during my mortal years, I would have absolutely gone insane. But not her. All it took was a couple of simple jokes and a stuffed elephant for that little girl to find a way to laugh again.

If I'm being honest, she's not exactly wrong about me. My face is a little gross and ugly these days. So are my arms. So are my legs.

I suppose my disfigurement should not be that much of a surprise, given the way I was separated from the mortal coil.

That's right. Once upon a time, I lived as a regular mortal, just like so many of the people who need my help today. Back then, my name was Roger Steinlin. Were you my neighbor, you might have thought I was the poster child for the modern American dream. I owned a beautiful three-bedroom, two-bath home just on the outskirts of Greeley where I lived with my beautiful wife Stacey and our intelligent daughter Olivia.

I made a pretty decent living working as a Real Estate agent in the Fort Collins area. For the most part, I was able to find my clients good homes well within their price range without too much difficulty.

Generally speaking, it's not that hard to encourage someone to purchase something they already want. You just have to find a way to cater to their needs.

Families with children just need to feel like they're in a good neighborhood to raise their kids, so I'd show them some of the local schools and children's activities.

For singles, I found the best approach involved mixing a little bit of harmless flattery along with giving them excitement about what this new home could mean for their lives. Bars, nightclubs, singles mixers...and of course, a thriving job market to build their careers as well.

For unmarried women in particular, I would often add in a little extra flirtation when it seemed appropriate. Usually it was just small stuff like a flattering comment or a playful tease. Sometimes, I added a bit more physical contact for added effect. A hug here, a kiss there, and soon enough I'd get them to sign on the dotted line.

Truth be told, I sometimes took it....further than that. A lot further. Far enough that Stacey would have rightfully divorced me had she known.

At the time, I rationalized my behavior through the lie that as long as I was bringing home enough money to pay the bills and made sure to spend some quality time with Olivia, there was nothing wrong with having a little harmless fun on the side with certain clientele. It made me happy, it made them happy, and it usually resulted in bringing extra money home for my family.

Besides, it was low risk. I worked under a different last name selling homes in Fort Collins, a city at least 30 miles away from where I lived, so it was highly unlikely news of any of my transgressions would ever get back to my family.

I felt invincible, like nothing could go wrong.

Time certainly has a way to make fools of us all.

It was a warm, summer afternoon when I first met a young divorcee in her late 20s named Amanda Richter. I can still picture the first time I saw her walking into my office, her long red hair draped perfectly over her back, accentuating the blue dress that held her perfect frame.

She had just gotten a decent settlement from her divorce and was eagerly looking to buy a new house to kickstart her new beginning. The energy she had towards her newfound freedom was invigorating, even if it was clear that she had no clue where she wanted to go next in life.

When I met her, she wasn't all that concerned about the future. Just being free of him and starting over was enough for her, at least for the moment.

During the day, I would take her out to see an array of homes I thought she might like. At night, we'd discuss each one over a bottle of wine at her apartment. No matter what homes we saw or what the price range was, she kept coming up with excuses as to why each house was the wrong fit for her. After a few drinks, the conversation always seemed to evolve towards mild flirting when she felt happy or offering emotional support when she felt at her lowest.

It was not long before I realized exactly what was going on. She had become a lost soul who was looking at me as her safe harbor from the world.

I don't recall which one of us made the first move, but I clearly remember the gleam in her eyes the first night we slept together. It was the first time I ever really saw her look comfortable and happy. I remember the incredible laugh and smile I saw on her face as she cuddled me tight afterwards.

Most of all, I remember the words she said as she curled her head up on my shoulder and kissed the center of my neck.

"They told me an amazing guy like you could never be interested in someone as broken as me.

They were wrong."

At the time, the phrase *broken* dug deep into my soul. Nothing about her seemed broken. If anything, she seemed like she had the world at her fingertips if she could only pick a direction to go. How could she ever see herself as anything other than the beautiful, adventurous flower that she was? Before I showered and went home, I spent a bunch of time cuddling with and comforting her, trying to show her how wonderful she was to me.

In retrospect, I perhaps should have spent more time figuring out who *they* were.

Our affair continued off-and-on for several weeks in between her short-lived attempts at dating. We continued to see each other at least once a week even after she purchased a two-bedroom, two-bath Bungalow in the northern part of the city.

At my request, we always met at her place. I claimed it was so Stacey wouldn't walk in on us, but in truth it was also a way to keep her in the dark about where I lived. If things ever went south, I did not want to give her an easy way to ruin my life. But I was always more than eager to go over to her place.

So when she called me up on a rainy afternoon and asked me to come over to get a "life changing surprise", I immediately grabbed my long, black trenchcoat and worn-down waterproof fedora before thoughtlessly making the drive to her house.

She met me at the door with a strong, passionate kiss and dragged me into the living room where she had a bondage cross set up. Before I could even take off my hat and jacket, she dragged me to the cross where I felt her tying my arms to the restraints. Then my legs.

Amanda walked behind the cross, muttering to herself as she teased my neck. My skin tingled when I closed my eyes and thought she might start trying to undress me slowly, but lost that thought immediately when she yelled, "you're wrong! He's here, isn't he?!?"

"Who-?" My question was cut off as she fell to her knees while tears ran down her cheeks.

"Shut up! You're wrong!!" Amanda's shrill shriek filled the room. "I'm not just his plaything! He loves me! He needs me!!"

I looked around the room nervously, trying to figure out what was going on.

"Amanda..." I struggled to speak over the sound of her cries. "What's going on? Who are you —"

She quickly stood up and interrupted my question by grabbing my head and sealing my lips in a nervously deep, passionate kiss. As soon as she pulled her lips off of mine, I could tell she wasn't herself.

"Roger, sweetie." Her face was covered in a

smile that was clearly trying to hide the sadness behind her eyes. "There's something we need to talk about."

"S...sure." I caught my breath for a moment, nervous about what was to come. "What's going on?"

"I love you," she stated with all of her heart, pausing momentarily for me to take in the news, "And I know you love me too. You've been so good to me for so long. But I know you want something more than what you have right now. I've seen that pained look in your eyes when you talk about your family."

My heart sank. This wasn't going where I thought it was going.

"I need more," she continued. "I know we had planned to just keep this casual, but...I want more. I need more. I just can't stand by and watch you languish in your failed marriage anymore. But he's right, you know? You aren't the type of guy to just pack up and leave your family. Maybe I can help."

Her eyes grew dark as her lips turned toward a frown.

"Amanda, sweetie," I pleaded, "whatever you're thinking, I...can't we just lie down and talk about this for a little bit?"

"You don't even know what I have planned yet," she countered, "but you will soon enough. Now, where do you live, my love?"

"I..."

The words caught in my throat as I tried to buy some time.

"Shut up!!" Her gaze left mine as she looked just over her right shoulder. "He wants me for more than just my body!!"

"Amanda, please. Let me down and let's talk about this."

"Do you love me?" Her eyes started to fill with tears, until she swiftly turned her head away from me. "Yes, I know he needs to be freed! What do you think I'm trying to do here?!?"

“I do. I do love you…” I felt the tears forming in my eyes. I wanted to reach out and embrace her, but the restraints on my wrists held me back. "Please! You don’t have to do this. Can we just talk?"

"If you love me so much," she answered as she turned her head towards me with a dark expression in her eyes, "then tell me where you live. Let me free us from the shackles of your family."

“The shackles of…” My mouth felt dry as the words tried to escape. “What…?”

The expression on her face told me exactly why I couldn't give her the answer she was looking for. As much as I wanted to hold her and comfort her, to be the man she thought I was, to be her safe harbor one more time...I couldn't bring myself to betray Stacey and Olivia that way. Not even for her.

"I see," she said while I was struggling to think of a response. "They're right, aren't they? You'll never give them to me willingly."

I nodded. She momentarily started crying, then her lips curled into a devilish smile.

"So be it. If I can't free you from their influence, then I have to free myself from you."

"Wait, I—"

She quickly silenced my protest with a kiss, gyrating her hips as she playfully pushed her body up against mine. A moment later, I felt her right hand slide across my cheek, then down across my chest.

"I'm sorry it had to be this way," she whispered just before I felt a sharp pain just under my chest, followed by the sensation of warm liquid flowing down my torso. "I really do love you, Roger."

I struggled against the pain to escape as I saw her walk to her bedroom and pull out a can of gasoline, dumping it liberally around the bungalow that she once purchased to kick start her new beginning.

"Amanda, please," I pleaded as she poured the gasoline against my struggling body. "Please! You don’t have to do this! We can work it out!! I love you! PLEASE!"

"I know you do, but not as much as you love them." She turned to face me with tears streaming down her face before giving me one final gasoline covered kiss. “Don’t worry. I’ll make sure they join you soon enough.”

“Amanda! Wait!! Please! Just hear me out!! We can figure something out!”

“Good bye, my love,” she said as she stood in the open doorway. “We really did have some good times together.

As she pulled away from me, I watched in terror as she lit a match and threw it on a gasoline-soaked portion of her carpeted floor before closing the door, leaving me alone in my last few moments to face my fears, my regrets, and the incendiary kiss of a roaring fire.

It didn't take long before the blaze intensified. My sensations felt frantic, switching between the heat of the fire, the smoke filling my throat and lungs, the pain of the stab wound, and the flowing blood that now coated my shirt and overcoat. My eyelids grew heavy. Before the darkness overtook me, one painful and solitary thought kept racing through my mind.

I deserve this.

CHAPTER 3

Even now while I sit in this stale hospital hallway on a lukewarm plastic chair, I can't help but feel a chill creeping up my spine as I remember that night. There was so much information I wrongly assumed I knew, so many things that I never realized I should care about. Things about Amanda. Things about my own family. Things about myself.

Hell, even the afterlife seems to continuously find ways to prove how wrong my beliefs in life were.

Something no one tells you about the afterlife is how you are dressed once you cross through the veil. It's not always white dresses for angels and birthday suits for everyone else. Most people tend to be dressed in exactly what they were wearing at the time of their death, though a select few people do wind up wearing items of clothing they were highly attached to in life, such as a favorite shirt or dress.

Whatever that outfit may tend to be, that is what their spirit will wear eternally.

In my case, I will forever be stuck wearing the

same all black outfit I wore that night when she tied me to that cross. Black trenchcoat, black button-down shirt, black pants, black belt, black gloves. I even kept the same weather beaten black fedora and the same knife that Amanda stabbed me with, though today that knife serves a different purpose resting at my side rather than buried deep within my chest.

Isn't it poetic that the very blade which once brought my demise has now become my instrument to protect others?

Speaking of which, I have a job to do.

With a sigh, I lift myself up from the chair to take my daily walk around the hallways, searching for any signs of Sorrowsworn activity. Most of the faces I see are familiar. Individuals who are haunted by their own thoughts, but not by the Sorrowsworn.

They can't see me. Only a handful of children have ever been able to, like the girl last night who saw my reflection in the mirror.

June Murphy. The newest resident of the Northern Colorado Mental Health Ward.

My heart skips a beat as I see her sitting on a windowsill at the end of the hallway, staring out the window longingly. She looks calm for the moment.

Without pause, I duck into a nearby wall and hide, hoping not to catch her gaze. If last night is any indication, I will need to help from the shadows so I don't scare her again.

When the coast is clear, I head to the nurse's station where Dr. Heaton is looking over June's files. Though the doctor closes the file before I can get much of a look, I at least now know that June has been admitted on a traditional 72 hour hold at the request of her father.

72 hours, starting from our encounter last night. Less than three days to unearth the root of her suffering, the core issue that attracts the Sorrowsworn to her.

That's not nearly enough time to do what I need to, but it's what I've got. If nothing else, maybe I can give her a few days of relief from the demons.

I step back into the hallway, peeking my head around the wall to see Dr. Heaton leading June into a nearby small office. Attached to June's shoulders sit two Sorrowsworn, one red and one blue. They seem to be silent for the moment, but a quick glance at their voracious eyes tells me enough.

They aim to feed. I aim to stop them.

I step into the wall and walk until I am positioned a bit behind the little girl, peering out just far enough to see her sitting in a chair across from Dr. Heaton. Across from June sits an empty chair.

I dare not step out any further. Since June can see me through the veil, I have to do it in a way that I stay hidden. If I don't, she'll be too focused on her fear of me to properly open her mind.

Not that she could see me right now anyhow. Her eyes are glued to the floor for the moment, clearly avoiding the risk of eye contact with Dr. Heaton.

"Good afternoon, June," Dr. Heaton says, staring at her softly. "I appreciate you taking the time to talk to me. If you are so willing, I would like to try to get to know you better."

"Taking the time? Like you have any choice in this, child." The blue Sorrowsworn peeks out from behind her left shoulder, a giggling hiss emanating from his lips as his body contorts in front of her face. "Maybe if you had been a good little girl, your family wouldn't have had to abandon you here forever."

Such sickening creatures. There is no depth of hell deep enough for a creature who would prey on a child's misery.

“They’re never coming back for you, are they? You’re going to be all alone here, just like—”

“June...?” Almost instinctively, Dr. Heaton sets her hand on June’s knee, capturing the child’s attention for the moment. “Are you here?”

The little girl sniffles for a moment before

choking down her tears and giving the doctor a small nod, fighting to ignore the demons for the time being.

I watch in the shadows as the two of them talk for a short while. The little girl opens up a lot more than I would expect at this point in therapy, talking at length about the voices even as they scream into her ear. She's strong, a lot stronger than she appears.

Still, the consistently lowering expression in her eyes shows how much the Sorrowsworn have done to wear down her emotional walls. Much like waves can eventually tear down a cliffside, the constant yelling and negative comments of the Sorrowsworn can break even the strongest people over time.

June is not nearly old enough to have built up a defense to them. The more they lie to her, the harder it's going to be for her to recover

The time has come for these two to go.

I slide closer to her, still hiding within the wall. Dr. Heaton looks up at me once...well, in my direction at least. She gives me a bit of an unexpected look, as if she is staring directly into my soul.

Wait. Can the doctor see me too?!?

I pull out my knife and wave intensely in front of her, making sure I'm in her line of sight and obvious. She immediately looks back at her notes without even so much as a flinch.

Guess not.

But the stone cold silence drawn across June's face tells another story. As soon as I look across the room, I see my reflection in the window. The red Sorrowsworn has his claws sunk deep into her neck, whispering something in her ear as his body shudders with laughter.

"Ooooo. Look over there. He's back, isn't he?" The demon smiles and lets out a high-pitched cackle. "The man no one else can see. The proof of your insanity. The—"

I answer the taunt by sinking my blade deep into the Sorrowsworn's neck, twisting until its demonic body disappears.

June initially flinches, then seems to strike a more relaxed pose as Dr. Heaton again grabs her hand.

One down. One to go.

"June?" Dr. Heaton asks, snapping her fingers. "Are you...are you still with me?"

June continues her silence, instead tracking my movements with her eyes.

I turn my attention toward the blue Sorrowsworn. He's still leaning over her shoulder, but has remained silent since his friend's death. In one quick thrust, I plunge my knife straight into the demon's chest, sending it screaming back to the nether.

The little girl involuntarily shrieks before returning to stone silence.

"What are you looking at?" Dr. Heaton asks.

"...he's here," June answers, still not risking her eyes leaving my reflection in the window.

"Who's here?"

"Him. The man in the hat. He's…"

"The man from last night? You see him? He's here with us right now?"

"Right over there."June nods while pointing a finger at me. "C…can you see him too?"

Dr. Heaton again gazes in my direction, yet I can tell from the look in her eyes that she doesn't see anything but air. Still, she nods with a smile before turning back to June.

"I wouldn't worry about him," the doctor answers. "Did you bring Raul?"

"I forgot," June quickly answers as she shakes her head no, her eyes sinking slightly. "Are…we in danger?"

"No, I don't think so." Dr. Heaton folds her hands in her lap, staring straight into June's eyes. "Even if Raul isn't here he can still protect us both from afar.

But...would you like to hear a secret?"

"Yes please," June answers, nodding curiously. “I’ll keep it safe, I promise.”

I am more than a little curious. What is the doctor getting at?

“Right now," the doctor answers while leaning forward, "you are the most powerful person in the room. You are stronger than anyone in this room, including the man in the hat."

The child's eyes light up slightly, though her eyebrows also raise in confusion.

"I know he looks scary," Dr. Heaton continues, "but have you tried giving him commands? I bet that you can control him. I bet that you can tell him to do anything and he'll do it."

What is she...?

"Want to try it?"

Oh...I get it now.

"Sure!" June turns her head towards me, her nervous expression turning towards a playful smile. "OK, Mr. Hat Man. Stand on one foot."

Without hesitation, I lift my right foot off the air, holding my arms in the air to push the illusion further.

"OK," June continues, lightly giggling as her face shapes into a soft smile. "Next, I want you to make a funny face!"

Again, I obey without question. My eyes cross. My mouth stretches wide. My cheeks puff out.

June bursts out laughing, forgetting all about her demons for the time being. Dr. Heaton laughs with her for the moment.

"Jump!"

I leap high in the air, nearly smacking my head on the ceiling. Not that it would be a problem for me, I'd likely just go through it. Still, I'd rather not show that particular trait off now.

"See what I mean?" Dr. Heaton asks, turning her attention to June with a smile. "For the next three days, you have all the power here. Not him. Not the voices. You, June Murphy, have all the power here. Wherever you are, he has to do what you tell him."

The little girl nods eagerly.

"So," Dr. Heaton continues, "when you want him to leave, just tell him to go to his room. Go ahead! Try it!"

Before she asks, I start to fade back into the wall, but stop once I realize June is silent.

"June." Dr. Heaton leans back in her chair, folding her hands in her lap. "Don't you want him to go away?"

"No," June answers, looking down at the floor.

"The voices. They're...gone. I don't hear them anymore."

I feel the area that once contained my heart warm as I smile down at her.

That's right, friend. For the time being, the voices are gone. As long as I'm around, I'll do everything I can to keep them from hurting you. And...if time permits, the doctor and I are going to make sure they never bother you again.

CHAPTER 4

For the next hour, I stayed in the room with June and Dr. Heaton, listening to the conversation. The child spoke in surprising detail about the voices she was hearing, including some of the harsh words they spoke. Dr. Heaton's face fell several times during the chat, clearly feeling sorrow for what the young girl had been through already.

Perhaps the most surprising part was how June kept looking up at me as she spoke with a glance that at times looked fearful, yet often seemed to be seeking my approval as well. I focused on her when she did, occasionally giving her a light smile or accepting nod when it seemed appropriate.

And of course, occasionally answering silly commands on request.

As the conversation ended and the two of them left to get lunch at the cafeteria, I realized that despite her continued fear of me, she was giving me a gift that I sorely needed these days: the gift of acceptance. So long as I keep the charade of being a puppet under her control, she might be willing to allow me to stay at her side.

For the moment, she has gifted me a token of her trust.

Such a gift should never be taken lightly, especially not from one haunted by the Sorrowsworn.

Back in my mortal days, I took gifts like that for granted. Between the innocent joy of my children, the loving adoration of my wife, and the excited flirtations of my affairs with clients, simple acceptance and trust was the furthest thing from a concern in my mind.

So you can only imagine how it felt for me to wake up alone on a rocky shore just outside of the Gates of Hell with nothing more than the clothes on my back, the hat on my head, and the knife in my chest.

In my limited experience, the first response most people seem to have at the Gates of Hell is not fear, but surprise. Some are surprised by the red misty sky overhead, others by how humid the climate is. To get a sense for it, think of a poorly maintained steam sauna without any temperature control or exits. Over time, the effect just grows in intensity.

Many people tend to just be surprised to find themselves there at all. After all, enough rationalization and excuses can make even the worst sinners believe themselves to be angels.

Not me, though. After a lifetime of infidelity and avarice, I knew this was exactly where I would eventually wind up. Given how I lived, it was well deserved.

Perhaps the biggest surprise was the overwhelming feeling of loneliness and fear. I was expecting to be surrounded by demons with pitchforks and the constant tortured screams of my fellow sinners, yet all that was around me was a surrounding feeling of desperation and emptiness.

Well, that and fear for my wife and daughter. After everything that Amanda had said on the night of my murder, it was clear that she would not just stop with my death. She wanted to kill Stacey. She wanted to kill Olivia.

She had to "free herself of" me, or so she said.

I had to find a way out so I could stop her...or at least warn them.

As soon as I was able to muster the strength, I got to my feet and pulled the knife out of my chest. Surprisingly, pulling it out didn't hurt. It didn't feel like anything at all. I took a look at the unusually clean knife and the already sealed wound in my chest before sticking the knife in the side of my belt.

Looking around, I found myself trapped on an island surrounded by a grotesque red ocean. The waves consistently crashed violently against the shoreline, sharp enough that they were clearly unsafe to swim through. At the center of the island sat a small brick-laden doorway leading into a dark cave. Next to the doorway stood a thin, muscular man dressed in a variety of black fur behind a podium as if he were taking dinner reservations.

He was looking right at me, gesturing slowly with his fingers for me to approach with a taunting sneer plastered across his face.

Not yet, I thought to myself as I flipped him off before walking away. Whatever fate he had in store for me could wait. I needed a way out and he was not likely to give me one. Besides, with the waves crashing so violently on this side of the island, it seemed logical that there would be an area where the tide was flowing away from the shore. If I could find it, perhaps that would lead to a way home.

This was not a place for logic. After several trips around the island looking intently at the shoreline, I realized there was no weak point in the water. No matter where I was, the waves were always crashing inward. Without a boat, escape by water would be impossible and there was nothing to build a raft with.

I looked back toward the man who was still looking and gesturing at me, now wearing a much darker wry smile. Unquestionably, he was taking joy in his job.

It was clear that whatever fate awaited me on this island, it would have to start with him. So I approached, keeping a hand close to the knife now at my side.

"Ah, finally come to see me, have you?" The man kept his eyes tied to his book, letting out a hissing chuckle between a few choice words. "No need to apologize for the wait. I have all eternity, you know."

I glowered at him, gripping my hand around the hilt of the knife.

"Hmph," the man said, looking at my hand on the knife. "You really think a little pen knife like that is enough to take out a denizen of Hell?"

In retrospect, I should have shown him the answer right there and then. Instead, I released my grip and stared.

"Name?"

I opened my mouth and tried to speak, but no words came out.

“Name...?”

I again tried to tell him my name, but to no avail.

"Oh, seriously. Come on, now," the man said, looking at me impatiently. "Name?"

Once again, I tried to speak. Once again, I failed to even get a sound to come out of my throat.

"You aren't doing anyone any favors here," he said in agitation. "Surely you can tell me your name, unless..."

The man started looking closely at my face, seeing the burn marks I didn't know were there at the time.

"Died in a fire, I see. Yes yes. I suppose that would explain where your voice went."

I opened my mouth and tried to exhale any amount of air I could, trying to force myself to make a sound. Any sound.

Nothing came out.

"It's not like it matters anyway. I know everything I need to know about you, Roger Steinlin."

He put a finger on my chest. I tried to back away instinctively, yet my body would not move an inch.

"I know all about what you did in life. I know all about your affairs. Mmmm, especially Amanda. And I know all about how you died."

The man walked behind my momentarily paralyzed body, putting a hand on my back.

"I know all about how your actions have placed your family in the crosshairs of your former mistress. I know all about how you want to go up and warn them...or even god forbid, save them!"

I felt his hand push into my back with intensity, forcing me into the open cavern. I fell a fairly short distance before I found myself locked in a brimstone lined cell. Above, the man was looking down at me, flashing a brighter smile than I knew he was even capable of.

"Welcome to your eternal home, Mr. Steinlin." He waved his hands as his lips curved into a mischievous smirk. "You will never leave, you will never escape. You will never be able to warn your family that she's coming. You will never get the chance to atone for the damage your sins have wrought. No matter what you try, there is nothing you can do for them now. Your role in their story is sealed. Their fate is out of your hands now and forever."

The man let out a dark, ominous laugh as he closed the stone plate overhead, sealing me into the cell.

"But," the man's voice said from an area behind my head, "I suppose it's not all bad news."

As I turned to face him, I found him standing on the other side of the bars to my cell, gesturing at two empty cells right across from me.

"If your mistress has her way," he hissed, "then I imagine it won't be long until your family is here, being tortured for eternity at your side. Mmmm, so many things I could do to them while forcing you to watch. "

Furiously, I tried to throw the entirety of my body weight against the metal bars trapping me in this cell, only to be thrown back to the opposite wall by an invisible force.

The man took a deep breath which he clearly enjoyed before looking at me with a satisfied smile, as if he had just eaten his fill.

"Tsk tsk," the man said as he walked down the hallway away from my cell. "Really, you have no reason to be angry with me, Roger. Whatever fate they face is from your actions and your actions alone."

CHAPTER 5

I didn't know it at the time, but that was my first experience with the dark deceit of demonic beings. They will lie, they will deceive, they will inflict physical pain, and they will drag every last ounce of delicious guilt out of you. They live to cause pain and thrive on anguish, often using the most devious half truths they can think of to get results.

In a way, their behavior makes an odd kind of sense. The demons of our world eat by feasting upon misery. Every ounce of pain they can inflict upon the souls of people like you or I is a source of sustenance. If they can latch onto the tears someone might feel from a breakup or rough day at work, it will give them the same savory joy as you might get from a candy bar.

He was just a hungry leech, like so many other demons such as the Sorrowsworn. He spoke to me in those same half truths so many other demons use, dining on my fear and anguish about how I had left my family.

That's the problem with half truths. Even if you realize that they are only half true, it can be hard to tell what half is true and what half isn't. And often the truth is the far more painful part anyhow. Had I known then what I know now, perhaps I...

Enough reminiscing. There's no sense in diving into the past when the Sorrowsworn are a threat today..

Despite how maniacal demons can be when searching for their next meal, the Sorrowsworn are among the worst. Most demons tend to only haunt adults, twisting everything a person does into pain for sustenance. Sorrowsworn on the other hand are all too happy to attack anyone they can, up to and including young children. Their half truths tend to be particularly painful as they craft their lies around emotional perceptions rather than actions, leading to most of their victims feeling a sense of overwhelming guilt when in reality they've done nothing wrong.

A quick glance at the door to room 227 is enough to remind me what happens when Sorrowsworn are left unchecked for too long. Not that I intend to ever go in that room ever again.

I can't fix the past, but maybe I can help June in the present.

Several hours have passed since the session with Dr. Heaton ended. Since the session ended, I have kept my distance in no small part due to the pain and fear I still see in her eyes.

While she was playful and inviting when all three of us were in the room together, out in the hallways she still looks at me with fear every time we lock eyes. I tried a few things to make her feel more comfortable such as standing on one foot and making funny faces, but all that seemed to do was make her walk away.

Worse yet, another couple of Sorrowsworn have grown around her in that time, filling her head with all sorts of self-deprecating nonsense. I at one point tried to reach for my knife to pop them, only for her to run from me.

As much as I want to help her in the immediate sense, disturbing the sanctity of her room would only serve to further deepen her fears.

Instead, I saunter my way into the relative solace of Dr. Heaton's empty office, preparing for a night time study session under the dim fluorescent safety lights that stay on at all times. Given the strong locks on the door and the fact that the good doctor went home three hours ago, I should be able to do most of my research relatively undisturbed, save maybe for the cleaning crew if I go too late.

Even then, I'm not too worried. They can't see me. The most they'll see is a few pages being shuffled around by what they'll likely assume is the AC.

Inside, the office is remarkably clean aside from an empty chip bag that just barely missed the trash can. The walls are all lined with books on pediatric psychology and medicine, though none of them appear to have even a slight spinal crease that would indicate use. The desk is covered with a stiff dark green mat placed conveniently close to a basket holding pens and pencils. At the center of the mat lies an open folder with records and notes for one of her patients.

I don't even need to read the name on the tab to know whose folder this is.

June Murphy.

It's almost too convenient, as if the doctor wanted me to find it.

Suspiciously, I take a look behind me at the still locked door, half expecting to see Dr. Heaton or another staff member. I'm alone for the moment, free to do my research without interruption.

Perfect.

I would rather not make my presence obvious. People fear what they don't understand. People don't understand what they can't see.

The first few pages of the file are mostly boilerplate forms. Patient intake, insurance information, medications, and a signed order from the doctor for a 72 hour psychiatric hold. Nothing really useful at the moment, though I make a mental note of her medications just in case.

Past that, there are a handful of handwritten notes from the doctor. There is a lengthy section about June's "hallucinations," talking about the disembodied voices she has been hearing. Oddly, the doctor specifically puts the word hallucinations in quotation marks, as if she knows that the voices are more than just hallucinations. Odder still are the three hand drawn stars drawn next to the note talking about June's worries about the ugly man in a hat.

Me.

Other than that, the notes are somewhat sparse. Some of the notes talk about her family life, both immediate family as well as what happened to her cousin Sebastian.

Additionally, there are also a couple of notes about her withdrawing from her classmates. Hardly surprising given what those demons have put her through.

I start to turn another page when I hear a doorknob twisting behind me. A lump forms in my throat as I shift my essence into the wall on the right, finding a spot just behind a tall potted tree to add to my cover.

I turn around to see the familiar visage of Dr. Heaton walking into her office. Damn! I thought she went home hours ago.

Her eyes turn towards the now scattered pages of June's file sitting on her desk. She lets out a soft giggle as her lips curl into a smile.

"Of course. I thought you might be here."

After glancing around the room for a moment, she grabs the pages of June's report before reorganizing them into a neat proper pile. Afterwards, she reaches into her purse and pulls out a small photo as well as Raul, the dirty grey and white stuffed elephant from the other night.

Both objects promptly find their way to the surface of her desk.

"Do you see him, old friend?" she asks. For the moment, I'm not sure whether she's talking to me or Raul.

Next, she walks over to the fridge and rearranges a small section of magnetic poetry on the door before grabbing a small bottle of apple juice. Afterwards, she blows a kiss into the office before locking her office door and once again leaving for the night.

Once I am sure she is gone, I step out from the depths of the wall to look at the items she left on her desk. Raul looks exactly the same as he did last night. Still stuffed, still fuzzy, still an elephant.

The photo is an image of June dated about two years ago smiling while being held by a black haired woman I would guess is in her early 30s. On the back of the photo is a handwritten note saying "Our Little June Bug with Aunt Rachel."

Curious...why would Dr. Heaton leave this here? Is there something specific I should know about June's relationship with her aunt?

Considering the implications of the image, I start to head out of the office, but stop when I glance at the refrigerator where Dr. Heaton was playing with magnetic poetry. Instantaneously, I feel the breath leave my body as I read her message.

I CAN'T SEE YOU

I KNOW WHO YOU ARE

HELP ME HELP YOU

ROOM 214

11 TOMORROW

CHAPTER 6

She...knows me. She knows who I am.

A chill crawls up my spine as I start to consider the ramifications of this news. All of that time I had wondered whether she could see me...whether she was looking at me. In retrospect, I had never really considered the reality that my visibility to her might not even matter.

She knows who I am.

What else does she know? Does she know about Amanda? About Stacey? About Olivia?

At the very least, she obviously knows that I was in her office, reading through June's files.

After all, she implicitly set that photo of June with her Aunt Rachel on the desk for me to see, right next to Raul who I guess I'm supposed to remember for some reason.

And she wants to help me...help her. Somehow.

Whatever that means, it's clear she has a plan to help June that somehow involves my presence.

I owe it to both of them to at least see my part to fruition.

Come what may, I will be there...even if I'm a touch nervous about where she wants to meet.

Room 214.

June's room.

Patients in this hospital tend to think of their rooms as their one safe haven from the world, their sanctuary away from the chaos that surrounds their daily lives.

Given June's fear of me, stepping into her room feels like a desecration of that sanctuary of safety for her. Once I am in her room, there will no longer be a place in this hospital that she believes I cannot tread. There will no longer be a place that she can escape to when she's afraid.

It's hard enough to face the demons she's had to face, let alone without the comfort of a safe haven to hide in.

I know that feeling all too well.

It's the same feeling I had when I first found myself in Hell, trapped in that diminutive cell.

That feeling of entrapment as the last vestige of safety you had in the world starts to close in around you, making your world feel like little more than an inescapable narrowing sarcophagus of fear.

When I close my eyes, I can still see that man walking in front of the surprisingly cold bars to my cell, boring into my soul with those fully dilated black pupils.

When I stand in an odorless room, I can still smell that acrid smoky stench of brimstone and burning flesh that was ever present.

When I stand in an otherwise silent area, I can still hear his voice coming from the desk he used at the end of the brimstone hallway, interchangeably weaving his taunts about my family's impending demise with maniacal cackling.

Such is the effect trauma leaves upon our souls. It echoes through time eternal, seeking to color every fleeting moment of joy with a recollection of misery and despair, draining us of our motivation to continue on.

Without a doubt, breaking my spirit and will to survive was the man's intent, if not the intent of Hell itself. The whole place is designed to break down every aspect of its inhabitants over and over again, wearing them away over time like waves against bedrock.

Whether I was in my cell or taken out for the occasional torture session, every last experience felt as if it was draining whatever remained of my sense of self. Be it the physical torture wrought upon whatever remained of my body or the mental torture of reliving my own death, I found my will slipping away moment by moment, ready to be resigned to my new eternal fate.

But the most painful part of the entire experience was not physical. Rather, it was hearing what the man said to me every time he walked me back to my cell:

"Think she found your family yet? I can only imagine what she'll do to them once she does."

Painful as his words were, within them I found strength. Every time he spoke, those same words served to remind me of why it was important for me to keep my sense of self.

I had to stop Amanda, or at least warn my family before she found them. If I lost myself to despair, it would just be a matter of time before she murdered them in cold blood.

No. I couldn’t let that happen. I would find a way out. Somehow.

My opportunity arose in perhaps the most unlikely of places: a long Sorrowsworn driven mental torture session. I was chained to a chair with four Sorrowsworn surrounding me on all sides, yelling taunt after taunt directly into my ears so they could feed off of my anguish.

"You don't love her. If you did, you never would have cheated."

"She deserved a king. You brought her nothing but death."

"Even if Olivia survives, she'll forget all about you in a few short years."

"Maybe it's better that way. Maybe the best memories of you are the ones she'll never have."

I wanted to scream at them. I tried to scream at them. But any time I tried to make any sort of vocal noise, nothing came out but air and frustration.

"Cat got your tongue? How's that going to feel when your lover sends Stacey down here and you can't even apologize for what you've done?"

My mind started to disassociate from their words, wandering thoughtlessly towards the sounds of the other Sorrowsworn in the room. The taunts they were saying to others were nothing short of horrific. Vile, ugly thoughts that felt steeped in half truths at best.

Near the end of the room, I heard a couple of them bragging about their most recent victims on the surface. The people they had feasted on. The tricks they had used. The savory flavor of each person's pain.

It felt like the most psychopathic water cooler conversation I had ever heard.

Yet I found myself listening intently to their tales. In retrospect, I'm not sure I understand why I focused on them so much outside of mere curiosity.

Still, as soon as I heard one of them talking about taking the path back to the "surface world," I knew I had found my salvation.

In that little window of a conversation, they had shared that there was a path between Hell and the "surface world." And all I had to do to find it was figure out a way to follow these two horrifying monsters.

I sat through the rest of the torture session, taking care not to think about my escape plan too much. I was still unsure whether these creatures could read minds or not, but I wanted to protect myself in case they did.

To this day, I'm not entirely sure whether they can.

Once the torture session was over, I walked on the man's right side as we traversed the foul horrid corridor back to my cell, keeping my right hand lightly on the hilt my knife in preparation.

Palms sweaty, I felt my heart rate quicken with every step. I had no clue whether or not the knife would even hurt him, let alone whether or not I could find the two Sorrowsworn I had heard bragging about their victims earlier. And that was before I had even considered whether or not Hell had guards.

It does not, thankfully. At least none that I saw.

"What do you think?" he asked, smug as always. "Think she found your—"

WIth a quick thrust, I took the sound of his voice out of his throat by replacing it with the blade of my knife. He fell silent almost instantly, save for the sounds of gurgling blood oozing out of the newly sliced opening as he collapsed onto the brimstone below. I had expected much more of a fight from the creatures of Hell, but was very happy to find out about his surprising mortality. After all the taunts and torture, listening to him struggling to take a full breath felt far more cathartic than I should probably admit in polite company.

As much as I wanted to stand here and watch him die, every second I spent watching was another second the Sorrowsworn could return to the surface and be lost to me forever. So I instead left him to his own devices as I retraced my steps back toward the torture chamber. I made it there with very little difficulty, due in part to the surprising lack of guards in Hell.

Even now, I can not fathom why the masters of Hell keep such little security in place. Perhaps they don't believe anyone can escape. Perhaps they just don't care.

In any case, I soon found the two monsters wandering along a path to the south, hovering distinctly towards the base of a tall, lava-covered mountain. I followed them at a distance, taking care to hide behind every large rock and shadowy corner I could find.

It was clear by their pace and volume that they didn't suspect a thing. They were simply content in their conversation and the anticipation of finding their next meal.

Once we approached the mountain's base, one of the demon's seemed to disappear into the rock. Curious, I sat back and watched as the other demon stared at the wall with a surprisingly jovial expression on his face.

"All clear," I heard the demon say as he peered through the rock. "Hurry, we'll have plenty to choose from if we can get there in time."

The other demon let out a light cackle before following their friend into the rock. As soon as I saw both essences had disappeared, I ran in after them, keeping my distance as I did.

The two of them took a windy path through the cave, one that eventually brought us to a bright light shining through a small crevice in the wall. It felt almost too easy.

I followed as they walked through the crevice, nervously wondering if they would catch on to my presence at any moment.

At the other end of the crevice, I saw several people sitting in the pews of a church, praying for salvation for any sins they ever had or ever would commit. The two demons started to approach a couple of the faithful, but soon found themselves on the sharp end of my knife.

Again, I had no clue whether or not my knife would even do anything. I got my answer as the two demons deflated like balloons while their life essence went back into the crevice, quickly disappearing from sight.

If I'm being honest, a part of me felt bad for the demons as their essence found its way back to the familiar surroundings of Hell. As much as I hated them, they had given me a gift that no one else could. They had shown me the way out of an inescapable prison. They gave me a real chance to be free, to find my family, and to perhaps save them from Amanda's insanity.

I just had to hope I was not too late.

CHAPTER 7

Start your day off right! Attend the church of your choice!

These were hardly the first words I expected to see upon escaping from hell. Still, the irony of the moment was not lost on me as I took my first real breath of fresh air since the night of my death. The wind carried the scent of rain mixed with a hint of sewage which ordinarily would have made me wretch, yet smelled far better than the acrid stench of melting flesh I had become far too comfortable with.

It felt good to breathe freely again, even if it was in the middle of the town Amanda once called the capital city of lonely misogyny: Wamsutter, Wyoming.

Looking back, it's somewhat fitting that my quest to find her began here of all places.

To that point, I had never truly understood her hatred for this small town. It's not that I particularly like the place, but it never seemed any worse to me than any other low population flyover town that overcharges you for gas and expired stale snacks before you leave it in the rearview. To me, it was just another podunk town in a mostly empty state.

But she...she absolutely hated it. Every time we took a road trip out to Yellowstone, she would become absolutely panic-stricken anytime we were near Wamsutter.

If I had only known the reason then, I would have absolutely handled things differently. If ifs and buts were candy and nuts, right?

Anyway, the first thing I did once I got my bearings was to go search for help. After all, I was still a good 150 miles from home and time felt like it was slipping away fast. Had she found my family yet? As afraid as I was of the answer, I had to find out.

It was not long before I came upon a tour bus parked next to the only church in Wamsutter. Can't help but see the irony of a town with only one church telling people to attend "the church of your choice."

Anyway, I found a group of teenagers sitting next to the bus in an array of lawn chairs enjoying the remains of a makeshift pancake breakfast. Hungry and hopeful, I walked up to a woman and tried to introduce myself, only to be painfully reminded once again that my voice was still gone.

Not that it would have made a difference

anyway.

Beyond just my inability to talk, it soon became readily apparent that she could not see me, nor did she have any idea I was there. Nor did anyone else that was around.

It was not for a lack of trying either. I tried several things to get their attention. Blocking the direct line of sight between friends. Jumping up and down. Bashing my fist against the side of the bus. Hell, I even tried to punch one of the chaperones.

The only thing I was able to really do was knock a plate of pancakes out of a woman's lap, and the only thing that did was make her get up for seconds and a wet wipe.

Discouraged, I was starting to consider what my next option might be when I heard an older man step out of the bus and yell out, "all right, folks! Let's get loaded up! Next stop, Greeley!"

Perfect. They were going exactly where I needed to go. Without a second thought, I walked past the speaker onto the bus, taking a seat in the back where I could be alone with my thoughts.

Soon, I would be home. Soon, I would know for sure whether or not my family was still OK.

I spent that entire ride terrified about what I might find. The fear of the unknown can be absolutely crippling, especially when it involves the wellbeing of people that you love.

As I stand outside of room 214 staring at the nameplate for June Murphy, I can't help but wonder if that's the same feeling that June's parents are feeling right now. That same feeling of helplessness, knowing that their daughter is in pain, yet knowing so little about the cause. That same feeling of powerlessness where you would give everything you had in the world to help, yet there's no reason to believe doing so would even make a dent in the struggle.

It's one of the reasons I take my job as seriously as I do. We have less than 36 hours to save June, there is not enough time remaining for me to squander hours here or there.

As promised, the doctor arrives right at the stroke of 11. It's relieving to see a doctor that arrives on time to a scheduled event, given how often they seem to run late. The grave expression drawn across her face reveals the fear she's experiencing before this upcoming gambit.

If she and I succeed at helping June, perhaps the little girl will get a chance to follow her dreams and live the life she so richly deserves. If we fail...well, I need only look at room 227 to know the price of failure.

"I hope you're here," she says, looking around the hallway for any signs I might be there. I try to move the leaves of a nearby plant, but it's clear from her sigh she gives as she knocks on June's door that my message was not received.

As Dr. Heaton opens the door, I stand behind her. June is facing us, hugging Raul close as she sits on the corner of her bed with a mournful expression adorning her face. She clearly has been crying.

Around her are three Sorrowsworn, all giggling as they take turns encircling her body and assaulting her eardrums. The red and blue ones are particularly persistent. The yellow one is quiet for now, but I don't doubt he's just as devious as the rest.

"Good morning, June." Dr. Heaton stares at her intently, offering a kind expression. "How are you feeling today?"

"Yesssss June," the red Sorrowsworn hisses in her left ear. "Why don't you tell the good doctor how you're feeling? Show her how weak you and that elephant really are."

Such vile creatures. The urge to charge into the room and stab every last one of them feels almost overpowering. I hold myself for the moment, so as not to startle the little girl.

"Better yet," the blue Sorrowsworn says while curling toward her right ear, "you could just tell her the truth. After all, she can already see that you're a FAT FUCKING FAILURE who will NEVER amount to ANYTHING!!!!!"

My heart breaks as June collapses into tears on her bed. Dr. Heaton rushes to her side, offering solace and comfort as she strokes the little girl's hair.

My blood boils as I watch the Sorrowsworn laugh and dance while they drink from her misery.

"Look what you've become," the yellow Sorrowsworn says, speaking for the first time. "A crying little baby with no one here to support you, except a paid employee. Looks like your aunt was right after all. You're going to end up all alone, just like—"

Holding June down in a hug, the doctor looks in my direction and gives a firm nod. Her plan is clear.

With the little girl's eyes hidden, I quickly dart into the room and pull out my knife, stabbing the blue and red Sorrowsworn before they can even make another sound.

I turn towards the yellow Sorrowsworn next., but hold myself back as I see something entirely unexpected in his demonic eyes: fear.

Interesting. It is not often you see a demon express fear, at least not overtly.

I can use this.

As the other two demons deflate and flow back into the nether, I stare at the yellow Sorrowsworn and wave my knife at him, taunting him further with every slow stroke I cut into the air.

"Are...are you...hunting us?" he asks underneath an expression of pure terror. "W...Why? What kind of a madman hunts demons? What do you—"

He goes silent the instant I put a finger to my lips. His eyes grow wide as my knife starts to tease the outside of his flesh while I take the finger away from my lips and swiftly trace a line across the monster's neck.

Sometimes, you don't even need a single word to get your point across.

His face crumbles as he cowers toward his fate, only to gain a small look of hope as my finger moves away from his neck and towards a picture tacked onto the far wall. It's the same picture Dr. Heaton showed me last night of June with her aunt Rachel.

"What? The aunt?" he asks. "Why do you want to know about her? Wait, are...you're here to feed off her too, aren't you? Weird. Wouldn't have taken you for a Sorrowsworn."

I press the knife a little deeper into the demon's flesh, reminding him what's at stake.

"OK! OK! Look, that's her aunt Rachel. If you're looking for a way to feed off of this little girl, memories of her aunt is the best place to start. I swear every time her aunt is brought up, June becomes an easier mark. And why not? That lady is an absolute fountain of hatred."

I nod at the demon, signaling him to continue.

"Weight issues, family issues, failure issues, abandonment issues...you name it, the aunt's probably said it. And since it's from a family authority figure, June internalizes the whole thing. However, the best way to get under that kid's skin is to taunt her about the sleeping child."

The...sleeping child? What sleeping child?

"So...now that you know how to get a feast, you hungry? I could absolutely go for some—"

I give him his answer with a quick thrust of my knife. He shrieks as I return him to the Hell he came from.

Better fate than he deserves.

I turn my attention towards the bed. June for the time being has calmed down and is curled up in Dr. Heaton's lap, offering a slew of apologies no child should ever have to give.

As she does, I begin to take my leave from June's room before she notices my presence any further. While this was certainly not whatever Dr. Heaton had planned, I have at least gotten some answers. I know who we're fighting, better than I'd care to. And I—

"Wait! Don't go!"

I turn my head to see June's tear reddened

eyes staring straight at me from the comfort of Dr. Heaton's lap.

"Please, sir. Would you mind staying with us for a while?" she asks. "The voices always seem to go away when you're near."

CHAPTER 8

To an outsider, June probably would appear to be just like any other young girl. Playful, joyous, witty, smart, and someone with a bright future ahead of her. From all appearances, she is a child filled with overwhelming joy and excitement.

Yet in this specific moment, her eyes are filled with an expression I know far too well: the agonizing glare of fear attempting to seek out a lifeline against hopeless desperation.

No surprise there. She has been fighting this mental war with the Sorrowsworn for so long, and the consequences of each battle have to weigh heavily upon her mind. Over time, they can wear on even the strongest souls.

I walk back towards her, taking a place to sit on the bed. It's clear from the way Dr. Heaton is softly petting June's hair that she sees it too.

Perhaps this is why Dr. Heaton wanted me in here for this. Perhaps she had already seen that look in June's eyes and knew not to ignore it.

I wish I had been so good about noticing that

look during my life.

The last time I remember seeing it was on my birthday, just about a month before my death. That night, Stacey took me to a local comedy show to celebrate.

I suppose we had a fairly decent time and a few laughs, but the whole event felt a little weird since the two of us had not really gone out on a proper date in years. Not that we didn't want to, but things just kept getting in the way. Raising Olivia, late nights at the office...and of course, my unfortunate habit of having salacious affairs with my clients.

Still, the night was memorable not just for the date and the look, but also for one of the most memorable quotes I've ever heard from a comic:

No matter how old you are, if a little kid hands you a toy phone, you answer it.

When I close my eyes, I can still feel Stacey's head cuddling into my chest as she looked up at me and said in a quivering tone, "you'd answer that call, wouldn't you? That's just the kind of father you are. I hope you know how lucky Olivia and I are to have you in our lives."

In her gaze, I saw that exact same look of hopeless, futile desperation. In retrospect, I'm pretty sure she knew that my thoughts that night were more focused on the sexy birthday surprise Amanda had been teasing me with than anything to do with my wife and daughter.

At the time, I dismissed her sad expression with a light kiss and a soft "love you" that my heart wasn't into rather than taking it to heart.

During that first bus ride from Wamsutter after my escape from hell, my thoughts kept wandering back to that moment, filling my heart with further regret. Had I only listened, had I only kept my fidelity to Stacey...perhaps neither she or Olivia would be in danger. Perhaps I would still be alive. Perhaps...

"Welcome to Greeley," yelled the driver from the front of the bus. "If this is your stop, please make sure you have all of your luggage and personal belongings with you."

I got up and instinctively stood in line to exit. It was not until a tall man walked right through me into the exact same spot I was standing that the reality of my insubstantial state hit again.

It seemed so rude at first. How dare he stand right on top of me! Did he not realize that I was standing right...?

He didn't realize it. He had no idea.

He couldn't see me. No one on this bus could.

Well, almost no one. As I started walking through the other people lined up to leave the bus, there was a little girl with long, blonde hair who was pointing at me while asking her mom, "look, right there! Do you see that?!? There's a man just walking straight through the entire line!"

Her mom dismissed it at the time with a simple, “no, Dawnie. There’s no one there. Maybe one of your new imaginary friends is in a hurry."

"My friends aren't imaginary," the little girl protested. "They're real people! They really talk to me! Someday you'll see!"

For the record, they were very real, though they weren't exactly people or friends. I doubt I need to elaborate any further.

As soon as I stepped outside, the outdoor aroma would have told me I was in Greeley even without the driver's yell.

If you have never smelled Greeley on a particularly hot day, consider yourself lucky. Every so often, the scent of the nearby slaughterhouse is picked up by the wind and carried across the entire town. It smells like the unholy mixture of sour milk and cow manure combined with just a hint of death rot.

My god, I hated that scent in life. Every time I smelled it, I wretched a little and wished we could move somewhere else.

Yet on that day the odor was almost welcoming me home. It was a sign that I was close to my family.

Soon, I would know if they were safe.

After finding the nearest cross street, I began to follow the map that had been burned into my brain after ten years of day-to-day living. I walked for about twenty minutes or so before reaching the edge of the neighborhood that I once called home.

My heart started pounding heavily as I slowly made my way down the streets, scanning for any sign of Amanda being here now or in the recent past.

Nothing here seemed to be out of the ordinary. Yet with every step, there was a certain sense of foreboding in the air.

One that built up all the way until I reached my driveway where I saw Stacey's father sitting in his car, yelling out to her brother Andrew who was frantically running out through the garage.

The moment I saw the two of them, my stomach fell. Particularly Andrew who last I knew was living in Missouri about 700 miles away.

"Any word?" her brother asked as he stepped into the car. "Do we know how she's doing?"

"No, nothing yet," her father answered. "Your mother and Olivia are at the hospital with her now."

"What about Tony?"

Tony? Her co-worker?

Her father shrugged as he put the car in reverse

and started driving. I took the opportunity to hop in the back and listen to their conversation, hoping either to overhear what had happened or how Tony was involved.

Given my worries, the ride to the hospital turned out to be more than just a little frustrating. I had so many questions, yet nothing in their conversation gave me any indication of Stacey's condition. I tried to get their attention once or twice, but nothing worked. I still was unable to speak, they still couldn't see me, and the only thing swatting them with my hat did was mess up Andrew's overcombed hair.

It was no better once we got to the hospital. The waiting room was filled with several members of her family, many of which I had not seen in several years. My parents were there as well, each adorning a contemplative look of sorrow.

I grabbed an empty chair next to them and tried to set my hand on my mother's left shoulder. She pulled it away with a shiver, instead cuddling further into my father's arms.

"I don't know that I want to stay here too long," my mother said. "Being here just brings back too many bad memories."

"It's hard," my father answered. "I miss him too. But you know he would have wanted us to stay in their life."

A lump formed in my throat. They were talking about me in the past tense, sharing memories and talking about what I would have wanted rather than who I am.

I was dead. I was nothing more than someone who used to be their son.

It's not like I had any illusions about my current state of mortality. After all, I had been in hell less than a day ago.

Yet hearing the way they spoke really drove the truth of my new reality home.

I was gone. I was...nothing more than a memory they once called son.

"We could go visit him after this if you like," my father said calmly. "Linn Grove isn't too far from here."

"Sure," my mother answered. "That sounds lovely. It's just...she's here too, you know."

"Who...?"

My mother answered him with a grave expression across her face, one that my father instantly understood.

Before I could contemplate what their shared expression meant, the conversation was interrupted by Tony, her old coworker. He was walking into the waiting room dressed in blue scrubs cradling a blue blanket in his arms. Why would anyone…?

In retrospect, I have to wonder if my mind was trying to protect me from the truth. A truth I found soon enough anyhow.

As I looked closer, I saw that he wasn't cradling a pile of blankets. He was cradling a small newborn baby boy.

Almost immediately, Stacey's family swarmed around Tony to get a good look at the newborn. My parents walked up to greet him as well, albeit a bit slower.

"Everyone," he said with a twinkle in his eye. "Stacey and I would like you to meet our new son, David."

Our new son.

No, not our new son. Stacey's new son. Stacey and Tony's newborn son.

That's why everyone was visiting her in the hospital. Not because she was in danger, but because she was in labor.

The feeling of relief was almost incalculable for me. She was safe. Olivia was safe.

A twinge of envy stung me as I watched everyone fawn over the new baby.

My family had moved on without me. Stacey had a newborn son. Olivia had a new baby brother.

Without a voice or substantial terrestrial body, all I would ever be able to do is watch them grow up without me, spying on their lives from behind the veil. They had no need of me anymore.

With a sigh, I found myself once again hearing the torturing words of my demonic jailor:

"There is nothing you can do for them now."

CHAPTER 9

Watching Stacey cradle her newborn felt almost surreal. She had not even been pregnant when I died, so for her to be holding a young baby boy now just felt wrong.

Had I not only been dead for a couple of days?

One look at Olivia showed me just how long I had been gone. The same little girl I remembered wearing diapers just barely starting to crawl around the house a few days ago was now a vibrant eight-year old with long, brown hair who was excitedly hiding her face behind her hands, then pulling them away with a giggle for her new little brother.

They all looked so happy.

It was not long before she asked to hold him. Involuntarily, I walked over to try and offer my help with the baby.

But as I tried to lift the baby from Stacey's arms, my arms went right through both of them.

Instead, I watched helplessly as Tony helped my daughter cradle her brother in her arms. He was right there at her side, adjusting her arms while showing her how to properly support the newborn's neck, offering her tons of support and encouragement.

He was doing everything I wanted to do for her.

He was filling the role I should have had.

I watched them for a while, enraptured in a twisted myriad of emotions. Relief that Olivia and Stacey were OK. Happiness that my daughter was already starting to become such a wonderful woman. Sorrow that I had missed so much of her life. Anger at myself for ever straying from my family for...what exactly? Fleeting affairs?

Yet underneath it all was a current of denial about my role in their lives. It was not until I saw Stacey pull Tony's lips in for a long, passionate kiss that the truth of this situation became obvious.

I was no longer necessary. And it was all my fault.

Though I paid for my sins with my life, my family had paid a price for them as well. My actions had caused a vacancy in my family, one that left Olivia without her father and Stacey without her partner.

Tony had stepped in to fill that vacancy. And from the looks of things, he was filling the role far better than I ever had.

Soon, I came to the realization that while my heart would always belong with them, I no longer had a place in their world. Whether or not I was still in their hearts as well, they had moved on. They deserved happiness. They deserved to have a life free of a long dead memory of the past spying on them silently from the shadows.

They deserved better than me.

Fighting back tears, I gave my wife and daughter each one final kiss from beyond the veil on their foreheads before walking out of the room and out of their lives for good.

As soon as I got to the waiting room, I found my parents walking into an elevator. I quietly snuck in through the closing door, watching as my dad stared nervously at my mom.

"You sure about this?" he asked. "Last time we saw her, you–"

"I remember," my mom answered, cutting off his words as she violently pushed the button for the second floor. "But you know I can't just sit here and do nothing. I have to know why she did it. I need to look in her eyes and ask her why she killed our little boy."

"Sonya." He looked at her softly, weariness coating the bottom of his eyelids. "Do you remember what your therapist said? About how our son made his own bed?"

"I know," she said with a snap, "but that doesn't mean he deserved to die! He never got a chance to fix this. He never even got a chance to ask for forgiveness or make amends."

"Do you honestly think he would have?"

Even now, thinking back to the tone in my father's voice as he asked that question stings. He was not wrong. Had I not died that night, I probably would still be having secretive affairs to this day. Maybe with Amanda, maybe with someone else.

I doubt I would ever have even so much as apologized or felt bad for it, save maybe to get myself out of trouble.

But while it's too late for me to apologize or make amends to my family, it's not too late for me to make my afterlife mean something. I may not be able to help myself or my family, but I'm not the one who needs help right now.

June is.

I look up to see June sitting up on the bed, watching as Dr. Heaton hands her a small magnetic whiteboard which has the alphabet written at the top, but is otherwise a clear canvas. Next to June are a couple of dry erase markers as well as an eraser. From the conversation, I glean that Dr. Heaton has given her an assignment to draw things that remind her of members of her family.

The little girl's tears have largely dried at this point, taken instead into the distraction of drawing a bright blue cat sitting perfectly still out in a lush fenced yard colored in green marker.

"I like it," Dr. Heaton says as she looks over the little girl's artwork. "Who is this pretty kitty?"

"Her name's Ariel," June answered. "She...she's a protector!"

"She sounds nice," Dr. Heaton says, kneeling at June's side as she catches June's gaze. "Is she your protector? Is she watching over us right now?"

"Well...no, silly." June hesitates to answer for a moment, hiding her response in a giggle. "She can't watch over us right now because she has to watch over someone else."

During my living years, I would have just assumed she was giggly and coy. Yet the yellow Sorrowsworn silently growing out of her back tells a different story.

"I see. Who is she watching over?" Dr. Heaton asks. "Your Aunt Rachel?"

June nods quietly to herself.

"Foolish child," answers the Sorrowsworn to June's ears alone. "She knows you're lying. You've already told her too much. They'll find him soon enough and when they do..."

June's body immediately stiffens up upon hearing the demonic voice trailing off over her shoulder.

"Are you sure?" Dr. Heaton says, catching the obvious new tension in the room. "You know you can tell me anything. I promise I won't get mad or upset."

June quietly looks up at me shaking her head with an expression of sadness and fear. I nod confidently at her before repositioning myself behind the Sorrowsworn.

"It won't be long now. Just wait until—"

The demon's words are violently cut short as the blade of my knife pierces his flesh.

Sheathing my knife, I return to June's side and place a hand on her shoulder, giving her an encouraging smile and another nod.

"Not Aunt Rachel," she whispers softly. "Ariel watches ov...er..."

A tear rolls down June's cheek as I see a green Sorrowsworn rise out from her back.

"Yes...?" Dr. Heaton asks as June starts to shut down.

"Traitorous bitch!" The demon slithers along her neck as his mouth slides next to her ear. "Can't even keep one little secret for your aunt! No wonder—"

A quick stab of my knife ensures the demon is unable to complete that thought.

"You can do it, June." Dr. Heaton sits back on the bed and gently caresses the little girl's cheek. "Focus on me. Focus on my voice. Who is she watching over?"

"She...I can't!" June's eyes turn down towards the whiteboard as she breaks out into tears. Dr. Heaton immediately pulls the little girl in for a hug, offering whatever support she can.

A legion of Sorrowsworn starts to emanate from June's back, looking to feast devilishly upon her pain. As quickly as I can, I ensure the only thing they get to taste is the rusty metal of my blade as I send them back to Hell before they can even stay a word.

"I can't!" June exclaims as the waterfalls flowing from her eyes coat the contours of her face. "She said…If she knew I was talking to you, she would just..."

"You can do it," Dr. Heaton interjects as she pulls the girl's chin up, locking their eyes together. "We're here with you. Raul is here. I'm here. This is your safe space. You are the strongest one here."

"You're wrong!" June's voice quivers in panic. "The voices…they're just so loud! I can't…"

Poor girl. The voices have abated for now, but she doesn't know it. Their attacks have clearly scarred her.

I move off of the bed and kneel before the little girl who has now collapsed onto the bed facing away from Dr. Heaton. She tenses slightly as I grab her hand, offering comfort as she struggles to fight back her tears.

As her tears slow and her eyes open, I meet her gaze with a look of confidence. She gives me a soft smile in return...well, as much of a smile as she can bear for the moment.

"They...I don't hear them."

I offer her a nod before glancing at the whiteboard, then return my gaze to her.

“Can...can I hold the whiteboard?" June asks amidst a series of sniffles, clearly picking up on the hint. "He keeps looking at it for some reason."

Dr. Heaton eagerly places the board in front of June's resting body without a word. I take the opportunity to move my finger up to the alphabet written at the top of it, making sure June's eyes are on the board before I start pointing to letters.

Y-O-U A-R-E S-A-F-E

"You are safe," June reads out loud.

"That's right," Dr. Heaton says. "You are safe here. We will protect you."

June looks back towards me, offering a small

smile before sitting up and bringing the board into her lap.

"I know what you think," she whispers, looking down at her lap. "That I'm the strongest one here and all that. But...you just don't know about…I'm afraid."

"Afraid of...?"

June doesn't offer her an answer, instead keeping her eyes on the board. I bring my finger back to the letters.

I A-M W-I-T-H Y-O-U! F-R-I-E-N-D-S F-A-C-E T-H-E-I-R F-E-A-R-S T-O-G-E-T-H-E-R.

June looks up at me, then at the board, then up at me again.

"Face…their fears?" she asks. "Are you sure?"

I nod at her.

"But..." June says, her eyes going back to the board. "What if the voices come back? What if my aunt gets in trouble? What if I'm just faking it for attention?"

I A-M W-I-T-H Y-O-U! I H-A-V-E Y-O-U!

"You have me," June reads, her lips starting to curve into a smile. "But...who has you? What about your fears? If friends face their fears together, then…"

My eyes lock with hers, yet my mind feels distant. Almost unsure of itself.

W-H-A-T F-E-A-R-S?

"I've seen the way you look at room 227," she answers with an unexpected smugness to her voice. "I've seen how you try to avoid it, try to pretend it doesn't exist. It's the same way I look at...I know that look."

I feel whatever passes for my blood pressure these days rise in my body. She doesn't know how much of a nerve she just hit. She doesn't know what's in that room. Who's in that room.

She doesn't know about what I've done.

"See, June?" Dr. Heaton asks with a new twinkle in her eye. "Fear is natural. Even he has something he fears. But we can help him with that."

"Really?" June asks with an unexpected spark of joy. "You think so?"

I look up at Dr. Heaton as I realize my most recent fear is whatever words she is going to speak next.

"Of course he will," Dr. Heaton answers, looking in my direction with a smirk across her face. "Friends face their fears together, isn't that what he said?"

June nods eagerly.

“I bet,” the doctor continues as I start to realize exactly what I’ve done, “that if you were willing to face your own fears with him, he would be willing to face his fears with you."

With a sigh of dejection, I stare at the little girl's eyes. The look she gives me is a look straight from the bottom of Pandora's Box, one filled with hope and victory despite being surrounded with a lifetime of fear and uncertainty.

With a sigh of regret and a breath of acceptance, I nod at her.

“OK, deal,” she says, throwing a light smile towards me. “But he has to go first.”

...damn it.

Of course she would have me go first.

Before I can think of a way to protest her request, the three of us are walking out of the door and toward my greatest fear.

CHAPTER 10

Room 227.

Even just the site of the sign on the door sends a small chill down my spine.

To anyone else, this probably looks like just any other undecorated doorway in the hospital. There is nothing that indicates to her who or what is contained within the walls of this room.

But as for myself, I can feel my very essence shaking at the thought of stepping inside. I know most of what happened to the patient in room 227...and worse yet, all that I've cost her.

"Think he's ready?" Dr. Heaton asks, kneeling in front of June.

My legs feel frozen in place as I stare at the door. I don't want to see what's on the other side. I don't want June to see what's on the other side. The poor little girl doesn't know about...

"You promised," June says, taking my hand in hers. "Friends face their fears together, remember?"

I wish I could forget. A part of me wants to just

run far away from this place and forget all about it.

I look down to see June looking up at me with a mischievous smile paired with a set of eyes guilting me into irrational courage.

For better or worse, I nod at her with feigned confidence and take a deep breath. I feel my pulse quicken as Dr. Heaton's hand reaches out to turn the knob.

I'm terrified of what awaits me beyond that door, but at least I don't have to face it alone. I have June, I have Dr. Heaton...and unlike the first time I visited this room, I understand why it all happened.

I just wish I could have explained it to my parents that day at the hospital when I left Olivia's side and followed them up to room 227.

The then, now, and future home of one Amanda Richter.

My mother was a nervous wreck as we stepped off of the elevator on the second floor. My father stood tall and confident without the appearance of fear, though his eyes told me a different story. Both had their attention drawn straight towards her room as we approached it nervously.

They had no idea I was there.

"I'm going to kill her, Harold. I'm going to kill her," my mother said as we came to the threshold of the door. "By the good graces of God, I don't think I can hold myself back this time."

"I get it," my father answered as he put a hand on her shoulder. "I don't think I will ever be able to forgive her for what she did to our little boy. But we have to keep our heads if we're going to do this. Killing her won't bring Roger back."

My mother shot my father an incredulous look filled with tears she had lost long ago.

"Maybe not," she said, her voice quivering, "but at least I'll be able to sleep knowing someone made her pay for his murder. I still can't believe that judge let her off with an insanity plea. The fact that she might someday walk the streets again is sickening."

Silently, my father pulled her in close for a hug, trying as hard as he could to be her rock as her emotions poured out onto his shoulder. A quick glance at his eyes showed an expression filled with the pain that can only be wrought by reliving a parent's worst nightmare again and again.

I tried to join in their hug, hoping that perhaps they would sense my presence somehow. Every so often, I find myself wondering if a part of them did, even unconsciously.

After they broke the hug, my parents both took one more look at the door before wandering back toward the elevator. A part of me wanted to follow them, to be at their side as they lived out their retirement years.

Yet, I could not pull my gaze away from Amanda's room. Perhaps I was looking for answers as to what happened after my death. Or maybe I just wanted a sense of closure.

Either way, I was absolutely unprepared for the visage that awaited me inside. Blankets and sheets had been thrown randomly around the room, surrounded only by an array of plastic drinking cups. Amanda sat on the edge of her stripped bare bed staring lifelessly into the opposite wall, humming a tune I did not recognize. Her arms were covered in various cuts, drawing a path towards her hands which folded weakly in the center of her lap. Her clothing was tattered with various claw marks as if she had been ripping at it. Her hair was frazzled and messy, and her skin had a sickly pale hue to it.

It was clear from the expression in her eyes that she had become the hollow husk of a woman who once had such a vibrant zest for life.

A zest I stole from her during our affair.

Even with her unsettled appearance, for a moment I could not help but find myself lost in the traces of the same beauty I had been enamored with just before my death.

Despite everything, she was still just as gorgeous and lovely today as when we first met.

"Roger?" she asked as her eyes blinked for the

first time since I entered the room. "Is that...is that you?"

At the time, I didn't have a clue how she was able to see me, especially since neither Stacey, Olivia, nor my parents were able to. Maybe she felt my presence. Maybe she could see me somehow. Or maybe, just maybe, a part of her always hoped that she would see me again.

For a moment, a part of me wondered if perhaps we could even start to try to mend fences. Yet in an instant, the illusion was shattered as a gaggle of Sorrowsworn started to spawn from her shoulders, taking turns shouting menacing taunts into her ears.

"Look at his face," one demon hissed as Amanda started to tense up. "Look at those burns. You did all of that to him."

"He never lied to you, not once," another one said. “He told you about his family. He told you about his dreams. But you couldn't help yourself, could you? You killed the only man who was honest and compassionate with you."

"The only man who EVER could love you for the ugly psycho you are."

My stomach sank as I watched her head sink into her outstretched arms, helplessly caught in the surrounding cavalcade of demonic voices and emotional misery.

"I'm...I'm so sorry," she exclaimed in between her tears. "I...love you. I wish...I had...never..."

The Sorrowsworn seemed to revel in her pain as her face fell again, feeding off every last sob and shriek that she emitted.

I wanted to leave. It killed me to see her in such pain.

Yet, I didn't want to leave her in this state. Sorrowful, haunted, reliving her past misery. Despite everything, she deserved better. She deserved someone at her side.

She deserved a chance to deal with her pain without all of these damn demons screeching in her ears.

Before I realized what I was doing, I found my right hand attached to the hilt of my knife and unsheathed it.

"Oh god! Roger! No!" She instinctively jumped back as I pulled out the knife and lunged towards her. "Please don't! I know I..."

With a flick of the wrist, a quick slash sent three of the demons screaming into the abyss as their severed remains dissolved into the air. Another slice and two more Sorrowsworn found their way back to hell.

"...do it," she said fearfully. "I deserve it. Just please make it quick."

Each time the tip of my blade found another demon, the drive to slay them grew more intense in my heart. It was not until the demons had stopped coming back that I realized that Amanda had curled herself into a fetal ball, cowering on the edge of her bed.

She thought I was trying to kill her. She thought I wanted revenge for my own death.

As soon as I realized what I had done, I stepped away in horror. Whatever my intentions had been, I had come at her wielding a knife without any sort of explanation. I had struck just as much terror into her heart as any demon had that night.

I had reinforced everything the demons were telling her.

I watched with stunned silence as her body left the fetal position. She looked around the room, searching frantically with her eyes. Soon, she found her way to her feet and started to pace back and forth as she wound her fingers nervously through her hair.

"Roger?" she muttered, stopping her pacing seemingly to stare in my direction. "Are...are you still here, my love? I'm so sorry, my dear. I...just..."

Without warning, she crumbled to the floor, her eyes filling with tears. I could not help but kneel before her, placing a hand on her knee for support as well as to get her attention.

But as her eyes darted around the room, it soon became apparent that whether she had seen me before, she could not see me now.

Yet she knew I was there, at least for a time.

"That was really you, my love. Wasn't it?" She stared forward with an empty expression on her face, seemingly speaking to nothingness. "Just now. You were here and..."

Her body tensed up as tears began to stream down her cheeks.

"My love," she said as her eyes turned toward the fluorescent lights in the ceiling. "Wherever you are now, whatever you are doing. I hope you know that I will always miss you and I am so, so sorry for everything."

CHAPTER 11

How long has it been since that day? Maybe three years, maybe five. It's hard to say. When you have no scheduled appointments nor a mortal need for the pleasures of sleep, passing time becomes little more than a barely noticeable social construct.

However long it's been, that day was the last day she saw me. I tried checking in on her for a while, even tried moving objects around the room to show her that I was still there. Yet after so many months, it became painfully clear that whatever she had clung to that allowed her to see me in the first place had died off that day.

That, or maybe her mind simply couldn't accept my presence anymore, so it blocked me out.

Whatever the case, Amanda never seemed to fully recover after that night. With each visit, she seemed more and more vacant to the world at large. Less aware of her surroundings. Less alive.

Even without the Sorrowsworn, she was getting worse and I was powerless to stop it. At some point, the thought crossed my mind that she was only here because of me and all I was doing was hurting her worse with each visit.

So for her sake, I stopped visiting. I never stopped caring for her or thinking about her, but I stopped checking in. Over time, the thought of what she was going through grew in my mind until...

Well, until now. Until the moment when a little girl reminded me of the importance of facing one's fears.

This very moment when she's tugging at my arm, more excited about helping me through my own fears than nervous about facing her own.

This moment when, after taking a deep breath, Dr. Heaton is turning the handle on the door for room 227.

As the door creaks open, June runs ahead, pulling me through the threshold behind her. Dr. Heaton follows us quietly, closing the door behind her.

My vision tunnels. My mind goes blank.

For the moment, my entire world revolves around two women: Amanda and June.

Amanda is sitting upright on the edge of her bed, her eyes fixated on the window at the opposite end of the room. Even from this distance, the look on her face is enough to rip my heart asunder.

She looks empty. Vacant. Broken. Regretful.

A far cry from the woman who had once been such a spark of joy in my life.

From the look in her skin, she has not been out in the sun for quite some time. I can't help but wonder how often she's even moved from that spot.

"Amanda?" Dr. Heaton asks. "Amanda Richter?"

Amanda doesn't give her the courtesy of movement in response, not even a blink.

"How are you feeling today, Amanda?"

June grips my hand tighter as her gaze shifts between looking at my former paramour and me.

"She's quiet," June exclaims after a little time passes. "Is this why you were so afraid of her?"

I nod.

“Amanda…?” Dr. Heaton asks again.

"I...don't understand," June says as she turns back toward Amanda. "Why would she scare you? I think she's beautiful."

She is, no question about that at all.

My eyes shift to Dr. Heaton, wondering what she will say next to either of them. Yet the next words to be uttered in the room don't come from June nor Dr. Heaton.

"I..." Amanda starts to say. "I...took him away. He's gone...because of me."

The crackling, unconfident tone of her voice tells me that these may be the first words she has spoken in a very long time.

"Took who away?" June asks, her hand pulling away from mine as she starts to move closer to Amanda.

"Stay back, June," Dr. Heaton warns, placing her body between the two patients.

"Him." As Amanda speaks that one simple word, her gaze turns towards the approaching child. "He was here and...now he's gone. Forever."

"Who?" June asks before pointing a finger at me. "Him? My friend?"

Amanda's eyes dart between June and I, the expression on her face growing more puzzled with each shifting glance.

“I…I don’t…”

"He's not gone," June continues. "He's just a fraidy cat. But that's what friends are for, right? It’s just like he told me. Friends face their fears together!"

June looks up at me with a confident smile. Hoping to mask my doubts, I look back at her and nod.

"That’s right, June," Dr. Heaton answers, backing off slightly to allow June better access. "That's exactly what friends do."

"Your friend," Amanda says with a twinge of regret in her voice. "He's...afraid of me...?"

"Yeah," June answers, taking another step forward. "But he's trying really hard not to be."

"He is...?," Amanda asks. "Do...do I know him?"

June looks up at me for a moment, then returns her gaze to Amanda after I nod in acknowledgement.

"He says you do."

"OK...what's his name?"

June pauses for a moment before shrugging her shoulders.

"Hey mister," she asks as she looks up at me, "what's your name again?"

"Roger," Dr. Heaton answers with an air of confidence. "His name is Roger."

I feel a lump grow in my throat as I realize I never told my real name to either her or June. How does she know my name? How much does she know about who I was?

"I...see," Amanda answers with a sigh. "So my Roger is..."

Amanda's sentence trails off as she looks down at her hands, fighting back an escaping tear.

"I...guess I shouldn't be surprised he's so afraid of me," she continues. "After what I did to him..."

Effortlessly, June jumps up on the bed, pulling up a spot next to Amanda. As I cautiously approach the two of them, Dr. Heaton pulls out the whiteboard with the lettering on top, setting it in June's lap.

"You can talk to him, you know," June says as her fingers run across the board. "Tell him how you feel. I know he looks scary, but he's really, really nice."

"Talk to him..." Amanda turns her head towards June, her eyes widening ever so slightly. "I...can't. I...don't know how."

Taking a deep breath, I walk in front of the two of them and kneel before I take June's right hand and point it towards the whiteboard lettering, hoping beyond hope that the right words will come to me somehow.

They do in the form of a favorite ongoing joke.

I-L-L N-E-V-E-R L-E-T G-O. I P-R-O-M-I-S-E

For a moment, Amanda stares at me without expression. Then, with a tear in her eye, she slowly opens her hand, pantomiming the scene from Titanic.

"It...is you. You're really here, aren't you?" she asks as she reaches a hand out towards me. I reach out, touching her hand with my own. Her body seems to tense up as I guide her down towards the whiteboard. "I am so, so sorry for what I did to you. I...I just..somewhere, I just lost track of who I was. Whatever happened, you didn't deserve to die."

Y-O-U D-E-S-E-R-V-E-D B-E-T-T-E-R T-H-A-N M-E

Amanda lets out a chuckle as she wipes a tear from her eyes.

"No, I really didn't," she responds, shaking her head. "I took you away from your family. I took away the best thing to ever happen to me. You should hate me. You should despise me. You should leave me here to suffer."

B-R-O-K-E-N T-O-G-E-T-H-E-R

Amanda looks into my eyes, her mouth opening slightly in shock. For a moment, I wonder if she can actually see me again.

Then, her lips curl into a slight smile.

"Broken together," she says softly as she pulls her hand back and sets it on the bed, "I suppose that is one option."

June and I both smile at her before I notice her gaze shifting over towards Dr. Heaton placing a clipboard in her bag next to that dirty stuffed elephant she showed me in her office.

"Doctor...Heaton, is it?" Amanda asks with a more hopeful expression in her eyes than I have seen in some time. "Do you...have room for one more patient in your schedule? I think it might be about time for me to talk to someone on a regular basis."

"Can you help her, doctor? Can you?" June asks, eagerly leaning forward. "Pppllleeeeaaassseee??"

Dr. Heaton's lips curl into a slight smile.

"Of course," Dr. Heaton answers, glancing down at the elephant before returning her gaze towards Amanda. "I would consider it a personal honor."

June cheers loudly as she turns to face me, the expression on her face the happiest and most alive I've seen yet.

"See?" she asks me with a wink. "Friends face their fears together."

I smile and nod at her.

She's absolutely right.

I just hope she remembers that lesson in a little while when the time comes to face her own fears.

CHAPTER 12

"Are you ready?"

June grabs my left hand and looks up at me from her chair as fear dances behind the whites of her eyes. I grip her hand tightly and nod.

"Remember, there's no pressure, sweetheart," Dr. Heaton says. "Just answer what you feel comfortable with."

June takes a deep breath and nods. As if on cue, Dr. Heaton leans back in her chair and pulls out her notes.

"June," Dr. Heaton starts to say. "During our last session, you started to tell me about Ariel. You said she was a protector, that she couldn't watch over Aunt Rachel because she was watching over someone else."

My hand squeezes June's harder as her eyes dart between Dr. Heaton and I, seemingly trying to find the courage she needs to say the right words.

A Sorrowsworn starts to form from the base of her spine. I prune it quickly before it can become a problem.

"Sebastian," June says almost in a single breath as her gaze fixates on Dr. Heaton's clipboard. "Ariel's watching over Sebastian while he's sleeping."

Dr. Heaton nods and writes a quick note.

"Sleeping?" she asks. "I thought he ran away."

As soon as the statement leaves Dr. Heaton's lips, I see the Sorrowsworn starting to swarm from June's back. One by one, I send each one back before it has a chance to become whole.

"That's what Aunt Rachel tells everyone," June says, her face scrunching up. "But I saw him once after he ran off, sleeping in the basement walls. It seemed like such a weird spot to sleep, but he looked so peaceful. I tried to wake him, but he didn't move. When Aunt Rachel saw us..."

The room goes silent as June's voice trails off.

"Saw the two of you?" Dr. Heaton asks gently. "What happened? What did she do?"

June's face goes blank as her breathing becomes heavier. She doesn't respond.

The Sorrowsworn start growing out of her back at a frenetic pace. One by one, I subtly slice through them with my right hand before they can grow while keeping my left hand attached to June's hand.

Clearly, we've found her core issue. Whatever

happened, if we can get her through this...

"You can do it, June," Dr. Heaton states calmly. "It's OK, sweetheart. We'll keep you safe."

"Aunt Rachel. She...she..." June's head sinks down toward her lap as her strength seems to falter. "I...can't..."

"Can't what, sweetheart?"

June shakes her head frantically. The Sorrowsworn begin to thicken, the swarm becoming difficult to contain.

"June, whatever you're going through, it's OK. Just let it out."

"No! NO!" June shouts. "I'm not supposed to tell anyone. Aunt Rachel...she said..."

"What did she say, June?"

"She said..." My heart breaks anew as tears start running down her cheeks. "She..."

The Sorrowsworn have grown nearly unmanageable now. At this rate, they'll almost certainly start taking over before too long.

With a sigh, I realize that I can't keep up. I can't trust my knife to hold them at bay.

I have to take a risk. I have to trust that this little girl is as strong as she appears to be.

With one swift motion, I move myself in front

of her and kneel. With my right hand, I lift her chin up, meeting her tearful gaze with a smile.

"F...friends....face..."

I nod, hoping beyond hope that June is able to find the strength I know she has inside.

"...th...their fears together."

After a moment, June takes a deep breath and turns her attention back towards Dr. Heaton.

"A...A...Aunt Rachel t...told me that he was hiding because he was extra tired, so we needed to let him sleep in peace," the little girl answers, stuttering over her words. "She told me that if I tell anyone, people might come over to take her away and make sure he never ever wakes up. That's why Ariel has to watch over him. To make sure he can sleep peacefully until he's ready to wake up."

Dr. Heaton leans forward in her seat, forcing the softest of smiles to shine upon her lips while she tries to hide the obvious pain she is feeling behind her eyes.

The cavalcade of Sorrowsworn surround her for the moment, yet hesitate rather than going in for another assault. It takes a moment before I realize the reason why: they know exactly what she's doing.

She's facing her core issue. She's facing her darkness. She's facing her greatest fear.

Soon, they will have no worse darkness to show

her than the darkness she has seen herself...and they won't have anything they can use to feed off of her.

"Thank you, sweetheart," she says as June fidgets in her chair, looking down at her shoes. "I know how scary it is for you to share that."

"It is," June admits. "He's just been asleep for so long. I ju—"

Her eyes sink as she pauses mid word, then her brow furrows slightly as she looks towards me before turning back to face Dr. Heaton. The expression on her face makes it crystal clear that she's just now realized the truth.

"He's...not waking up, is he?"

Dr. Heaton shakes her head somberly before the two of us wrap June in a hug, letting the little girl cry freely against our chests. Every tear that leaves her eyes takes the veil off of another lie she's been told, another lie she's been forced to keep quiet.

A lie that eventually would have swallowed her whole.

The Sorrowsworn around us step away, slinking into the walls one by one. They know they no longer have anything to gain from tormenting her. June has found her strength.

By the time her tears dry, the police will be here and June will tell them everything about Sebastian and Aunt Rachel. Dr. Heaton and I will be right at her side the whole time to offer any support we can, but I doubt she'll need it anymore. She's stronger than she knows.

She may struggle to get the words out at times, but I have no doubt she'll find the strength to tell them the truth before the day is done.

She's already faced her worst demons and held her own.

She's already faced her greatest fear and found a way to move past it.

Plus, she gave me the push I needed to face my own greatest fear. Without her, I probably would have spent the rest of my time here afraid of Amanda and room 227.

Odds are June will never realize quite what and incredible gift she has given to me. In time, she may forget who I am as so many other children have in the past. But in my heart, she will always be a true friend.

And as she taught me not too long ago, friends always face their fears together.

EPILOGUE

A cool breeze brushes against my face as I stand on the front porch of an unfamiliar house. Back in my mortal day, a gust like this would have blown my hat right off of my head. Yet tonight, it simply serves to bring one question: how many years has it been since I last left the confines of that hospital?

Certainly far more than just a year. Maybe five years? Maybe ten?

However long it's been, I need to start going out more often. I've missed out on way too many of the simple pleasures of life since my death.

Inside, June is cuddled up with her family, enjoying an array of well deserved cuddles and hugs. It has probably been a couple of hours since she last laid eyes on me, even though she has looked in my general direction several times. I suspect she can't see me anymore.

It's for the best. I've served my purpose. Now, she needs the love of her family.

On the other side of the living room, Aunt Rachel is sitting in a chair with handcuffs on, listening to an officer read off her Miranda Rights. She is surrounded by a handful of officers and a couple of Sorrowsworn sitting on her shoulders.

Given what she's about to go through, they may be looking at her for their next meal.

Downstairs, I hear the sounds of sledgehammers repetitively pounding against drywall, likely looking for Sebastian's corpse.

Dr. Heaton is standing next to me on the porch, shifting her attention between watching the action in the room, taking sips of tea from her portable travel mug, and glancing occasionally at that same dirty, stuffed elephant.

For the death of me, I can't help but wonder what she'll ever see in that du—

"Perfect," she says as her eyes lift from the stuffed toy. "I was hoping you would be here. Seeing June doing so well...I can't help but think back to the day I first met my childhood hero. I wonder sometimes if he still remembers who I am. Do you think he ever thinks back to that day when we first met?"

I tilt my head in confusion as she looks in my general direction.

"When I was a little girl, I used to see people that no one else could see. I used to hear voices that no one else could hear. Every time they spoke, I found the fur of my stuffed animals would always stand just a little taller. It's like they were afraid of the mysterious voices as well."

She holds the elephant up towards me. She's right, its fur is standing taller as if it's experiencing some sort of static cling around my presence.

She lets out a chuckle as she takes a sip from her travel mug, her eyes still looking through me rather than at me.

"As a child, my parents thought I was talking about imaginary friends. When I became a teenager, they assumed I was crazy and sent me to a psychiatric hospital rather than accepting the truth...that I was seeing and hearing something they couldn't."

She sets the cup and elephant down on a nearby table before continuing.

"One of those people I saw was a silent man dressed in all black who always wore a long, froopy hat. His name was Roger, as I recall. Tell you the truth, I was afraid of him at first. It’s not everyday you see a man leave a bus by walking through other people like a ghost. But I saw him again during a 72-hour stay locked in the hospital. For all my fears, that man quickly became my constant companion and best friend. Throughout that whole weekend, he was the only person who truly wanted to listen to me rather than tell me I was wrong. He was the only person who wanted to learn about who I was rather than tell me who wasn't there. He was the only person who treated me like an equal human being rather than a psychotic child. When he was around, the voices all went quiet and I felt like I could be myself."

My gaze shifts down towards the stuffed elephant, then back up at her.

"You know what he and I used to play with a lot? Magnetic poetry," she continues. "It's how he told me his name. That man, he never even spoke a word to me, yet always knew exactly what to say at just the right time. I still remember him setting Raul in front of me before telling me to 'face the elephant in the room.' To this day, this little elephant goes everywhere with me. He reminds me to look directly at the things that are bothering me, even if they're too scary or painful for others to face."

A single tear starts to form in her eye. She doesn't wipe it away.

"Looking back, the saddest part of that weekend was the end," she states, her voice cracking slightly. "After the voices were gone, that man disappeared with them. I missed him so much. Believe it or not, I spent years looking for him in every place I could think to try, but he was never there. For the longest time, I had no other recourse but to wonder: where did he go...and why? Why would he help me through my roughest moments, then disappear from my life just as things were getting better?"

My gaze turns from the elephant back towards her.

"I think I finally understand what happened," she explains, her lips curling into a slight smile. "These people you help...they can only see you when they need you, can't they? Once they recover, they can't see you anymore."

I...never thought about it that way. She might be onto something.

"God," she continues, "that has to be such a blessing and a curse. You do so much to help people who are haunted, yet never get to partake in any of the celebratory parts of life with them once they are free. I can't even imagine how hard that is."

Dr. Heaton's expression softens as she reaches for another sip of her tea.

Right. Dr. Heaton.

Dr. Dawn Heaton.

Of course it's her.

How did I miss it for so long?

Sweet little Dawnie, the girl who slept every night cuddling that same dirty stuffed elephant close, has now grown up and become an incredible doctor.

She really has come such a long way since we

first met. I can’t help but be proud.

"I know you can't answer, Roger. I don't even know if you’re actually here," she states, glancing momentarily at Raul. "But if you are, thank you for everything. Thank you for helping me become who I am today. Thank you for helping out June and so many other children like us. I don't know if any of us can ever repay you for all that you've done, but I hope that helping Amanda can give you some comfort as well."

I feel my face go flush, a sensation I have not felt since the days I had blood running through my veins.

She...remembers me.

After all these years, she still remembers me.

She even took the time to thank me. I wish I could thank her in the same way for all that she's given me over the last couple of days.

She looks over towards me with a curious expression. This time, it's not the look of a doctor trying to see someone that isn't there. It's the look of a woman looking into the eyes of a long lost friend for the first time in years.

"I guess I should probably go in and see how June's doing," she says, picking up her cup and Raul before walking towards the still open front door. "Say...when we get back to the hospital, I think you should visit the new nurse we hired recently who works in the Maternity ward on the fourth floor. Her name's Olivia Steinlin. Really sweet girl with a bright future ahead of her. She reminds me a lot of you."

NOTE FROM THE AUTHOR

Before I get into anything else, I just wanted to give a quick thank you to you, the reader, for reading *The Man in the Froopy Hat.* I greatly appreciate the support!

One of the better internet rabbit holes to go down is the Shadow People. If you have not heard of Shadow People before, it's a phenomenon where people from various cultures over the years have described seeing unknown beings that resemble human beings entirely wrapped in shadow.

Among the most famous of these Shadow People is a being known as the "Hat Man." He is a shadowy being who is known for wearing a long brimmed hat as well as a black trenchcoat. Some people describe him as featureless though others describe him as "scarred."

My first experience with the Hat Man was in college. I was hanging out with a good friend when they pointed at the corner of a gymnasium and asked me if I saw someone standing over there. At the time, I saw no one, but I was still very curious.

They told me they saw a man brandishing a knife who was dressed in all black and wore a large, "froopy" hat.

After a bit of conversation, he seemed to disappear into the wall without a second thought. At the time, I thought that was the end of it.

Yet a few weeks later, another friend mentioned seeing that same figure in a different area. This was a different friend who had never met the first one...yet they also were seeing the same person. He was still dressed in black, still had the same knife, and still had a large, beat up, "froopy" hat.

Before long, another friend saw him in another location. Same description, same hat, same everything. Then another friend told me about him, and another after that. Different friends who didn't know each other, all seeing the same person.

From all accounts, he never seemed particularly dangerous or aggressive, just scary.

For years, the aftermath of hearing all these stories has led me to a handful of questions: who exactly is this mysterious hat man? What purpose does he have for showing up when he does, and why are only a select few people able to see him? If he isn't here to threaten the people he visits, then who exactly is he waving the knife at? And what led him to this life of random apparition?

This book is my way of trying to find some answers to these questions.

Thank you again for reading *The Man in the Froopy Hat*. I hope you enjoyed reading it as much as I enjoyed writing it.

Sincerely,

Tanner Howsden

CHARACTER APPEARANCE BY CHAPTER

Roger Steinlin/The Man in the Froopy Hat
All Chapters & Epilogue

Amanda Richter
Chapters: 2, 10, 11

Dr. Dawn Heaton
Chapters: 1, 3, 5, 7, 8, 9, 10, 11, 12, Epilogue

June Murphy
Chapters: 1, 3, 7, 9, 10, 11, 12, Epilogue

Roger's Parents
Chapters: 8, 9, 10

Stacey & Olivia Steinlin
Chapters: 8, 9

The Unnamed Demon
Chapters: 4, 6

BOOKS BY THIS AUTHOR

Cora Christensen

After receiving a threatening phone call, a trans woman finds herself in the middle of a nightmare.

Cursive Letter G

Gabe is a special education student who has just been given a difficult task by his teacher - write a cursive letter G!

Katydids & Fisher Cats

A woman moves into a new neighborhood and hears a secret from a small child that will change her life forever.

Omen Bears

A woman in labor starts to have horrifying images of her child's future.

Ryxal & Zylaverse

Two struggling former high school acquaintances rediscover each other over gaming.

Vote For Aidan

In 2036, an AI runs for President of the United States.

Yara

A young woman caring for her sick father learns that her past involves a legacy lost to time.

ABOUT THE AUTHOR

Tanner Howsden

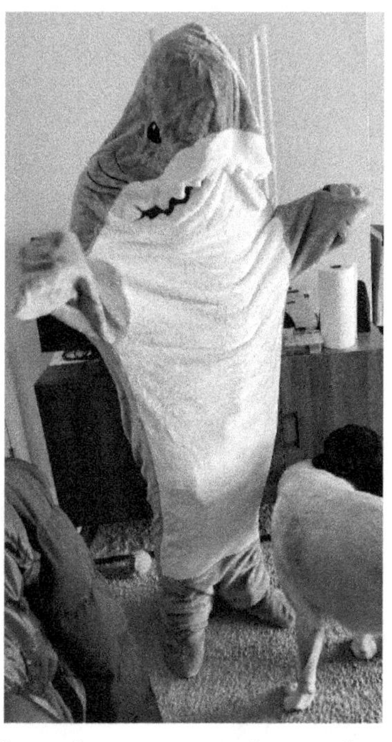

World famous author, renowned adventurer, philanthropist wizard, bovine hypnotist, billionaire playboy...these are all things Tanner Howsden would like to be someday.

In the meantime, he is a software developer who enjoys the art of creation. He has created a handful of video games and wrote the book you are holding right now. Additionally, he has had on-camera roles in a web series, a dating show, a movie, and a music video.

www.ingramcontent.com/pod-product-compliance
Lightning Source LLC
LaVergne TN
LVHW010930110826
845149LV00013B/2531